W9-BXX-021

 "Sam." Brynna touched Sam's shoulder before she could hurry off.

Sam stopped. "What aren't you telling me about the colt?"

"Maybe nothing. Maybe Dr. Scott's just grown too close to his patient." Brynna forced a smile.

Sam waited.

Finally Brynna rushed on, "I haven't seen the colt since you have, but he may be completely unadoptable. Sam, from what Glen tells me, the colt's not only disfigured—he's crazy."

Read all the books about the

# Phantom Stallion

# Phantom Stallion

## ~ 18 ~
### Firefly

TERRI FARLEY

AVON BOOKS

*An Imprint of HarperCollinsPublishers*

Avon is a registered trademark of HarperCollins Publishers.

Firefly

Copyright © 2005 by Terri Sprenger-Farley

All rights reserved. Printed in the United States of America.

No part of this book may be used or reproduced in any manner whatsoever without written permission except in the case of brief quotations embodied in critical articles and reviews. For information address HarperCollins Children's Books, a division of HarperCollins Publishers, 1350 Avenue of the Americas, New York, NY 10019.

www.harperchildrens.com

Library of Congress Catalog Card Number: 2004099837

ISBN-10: 0-06-075846-5 — ISBN-13: 978-0-06-075846-2

❖

First Avon edition, 2005

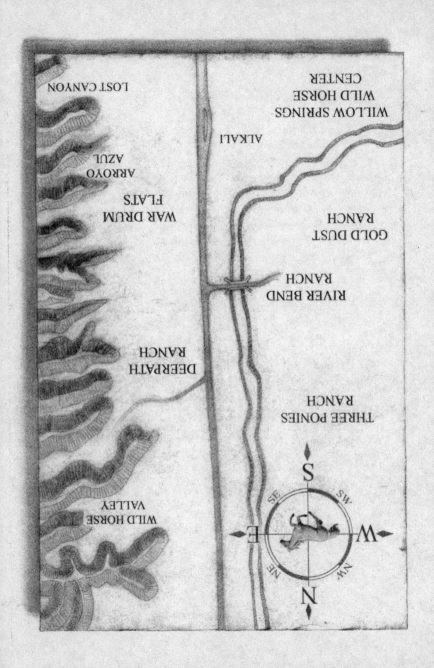

## Chapter One

Samantha Forster dug her fingers past the crust of garden soil, cooked hot by the August sun. She felt the cool dirt at the base of a plant. Was it a weed? She really hoped so.

Gram had assigned her to clear the vegetable garden of weeds, hinting that early morning was a good time to get started.

In shorts and a tank top instead of her usual boots and jeans, Sam worked in the shade of her white house, headquarters of River Bend Ranch.

Sam had awakened thinking of the river walk she'd take this morning with her foal Tempest. Her dreams had been filled with the splashing of tiny black hooves in the La Charla River shallows.

Sam hummed along with songs floating from the radio Gram had left on the porch. She felt cooler just picturing the wading horses, until the disc jockey broke into her daydream.

"If you're within the sound of my voice, brace yourself for the hottest week of the year. We're looking at a record 106 degrees by midweek and I call that a scorcher—hot enough to fry an egg on the sidewalk, I'll betcha!"

Sam wiped her forehead with the back of one dirty hand.

"Only someone sitting in an air-conditioned studio could sound so cheerful," she grumbled to Blaze, who lay beside her as she knelt in Gram's garden.

The Border collie raised his head from between his paws, panted in agreement, then returned to his doze.

Snorts and squeals, the clacking of teeth and thump of hooves came from the ten-acre pasture. The saddle horses felt the high desert heat gathering. For several days, most of them had stood under the cottonwood tree at the far end of the enclosure. Now, their pent-up energy erupted in crankiness.

Shading her eyes, Sam searched the pasture for Popcorn.

The albino gelding stood apart from the others. His white tail swished at flies as he watched Penny, another captive mustang, enjoy pats and coddling from Brynna, Sam's stepmother.

Would the soaring temperatures affect Popcorn's usual calm with this week's HARP girls? The Horse and Rider Protection program brought at-risk girls together with captive mustangs. Though Sam thought it was a great program and believed River Bend Ranch was lucky to be part of it, the girls could be—how had Brynna put it?—oh yeah, a *challenge*.

A porch board squeaked and Sam looked up to see Gram fanning herself with the hem of her red apron.

On hot days like this, Gram began cooking in predawn darkness so she didn't have to turn on the oven later. As Sam rolled out of bed this morning, the aromas of fresh bread, brownies, cheddar cheese, and chili peppers had wafted up the stairs.

Flushed but satisfied, Gram said, "Baking's finished and the *chili con queso* is just simmering in the Crock-Pot. I'm about done for the—Samantha, no!"

Sam snatched her hand back from the dirt and scrambled to her feet. What had Gram seen? A snake, scorpion, spider?

"That's better," Gram said. "If you hadn't loosened your death grip on my morning glory vine, you would have uprooted it, instead of that weed," Gram said.

"Sorry," Sam apologized. She almost wished a venomous pest had been skulking around her fingertips. She probably could have left off weeding for the day.

"The point is to pull out the weeds that are gulping up the precious little water we can give the plants," Gram explained.

"Okay," Sam said, though the explanation didn't help much. To her, weeds and flowers looked a lot alike.

Green and spindly, they crawled over the dirt, then slung slender tendrils around the wire trellis Gram had put up. Higher up, the morning glories bloomed with blue, trumpet-shaped flowers, but when they were getting started, they looked just like the weeds.

"I know they all look alike at first," Gram said. "You have to learn to tell the difference. Water's precious. I save it for the tomatoes and green beans, corn and strawberries, because we can eat them."

"What about the roses?" Sam asked. She'd been thinking they were purely ornamental, but as soon as the words were out, she thought of Gram's rose hip tea.

"The roses are something of a luxury," Gram admitted. "Though my rose hip tea is full of vitamin C, and it's the quickest way to cure a cold." She looked at the trellis almost tenderly. "But the morning glories don't ask for much and they keep showing up on their own. Seems like the least we can do is clear away the weeds."

Sam nodded, but she still didn't really get it. Her only hope was to memorize the ones Gram pointed out as weeds.

Cackling and squawking, three Rhode Island Red hens flapped up a dust cloud nearby. Sam thought they were squabbling over the cracked corn she'd scattered for them earlier, until she heard Brynna's voice.

"You feel up to seeing the mustang colt from the Deerpath fire?"

Sam glanced up as Brynna walked toward her. With her hair pulled back in its usual red braid, and a sleeveless white blouse hanging loose over jeans, she looked more like a teenager than the manager of a government agency.

Brynna had been the boss at Willow Springs Wild Horse Center for three years. She acted as guardian and overseer of the wild horses that roamed the thousands of acres surrounding River Bend Ranch.

Brynna didn't look like anyone's pregnant step-mother, either, Sam thought, but she was that, too.

"What do you mean, 'feel up to it'?" Sam asked, flipping back the auburn bangs that were already stuck to her forehead with sweat.

"He got some pretty nasty burns," Brynna said carefully.

Instantly Sam thought of the Phantom, and her stomach dipped.

Two horses had been hurt the day that lightning sparked a fire, which had blackened twenty acres of ranch land and heated the cans of paint sitting next to Mrs. Allen's fence to the point of exploding.

Sam had been following Mrs. Allen's directions, but she'd been the one who'd left those cans there. She still felt guilty for the horses' injuries.

The Phantom, a graceful silver stallion that had once been hers, had been temporarily deafened by the concussion of the exploding paint cans. He'd been burned, too, and the scorched place on his neck had turned shriveled and dark. It had looked exactly like a burned marshmallow.

The Phantom had been injured as he'd raced after a youngster from his herd. He'd tried to herd the yearling out of danger, but he'd been too late.

The yearling had suffered burns all over his face.

Sam winced in sympathy for the young horse, but she'd seen injured animals before. Of course she was up to seeing the colt. She owed it to him and because of Brynna, she might even have a chance to help him.

As the federal government's local representative in charge of the wild horses' welfare, Brynna had authorized expensive veterinary care for the colt.

"The last time we saw him," Sam said, "his face was mainly swollen from smoke inhalation. That's got to have gone down by now, and probably, that made him look worse."

"I'm sure," Brynna said. "But—" Brynna stopped speaking.

As Brynna broke off, Sam recognized the look in her stepmother's eyes. Most of the time, especially when it came to horses, Brynna treated Sam as an adult. Brynna was a biologist, and though she loved animals, she wasn't sentimental about them. She usually told the truth straight out.

"There's no point in trying to fool yourself, Sam. His burned nose and the damage to that white patch around his eye have changed his appearance."

"I know," Sam said, and her memory brought back the time she'd spent crouched beside the colt. A black crust had replaced the tender skin on the colt's nose. The patch of white hair around one eye had burned away, leaving behind skin that looked scarlet with sunburn. But damage done by flames wouldn't fade like sunburn.

*Poor Pirate.*

She'd never used the nickname aloud, but the bay colt's swaggering boldness, paired with his unusual white marking, had made her call him Pirate.

She'd seen him for the first time on Dad and Brynna's wedding day, the morning he'd caused the Phantom's herd to nearly trample her. Still, it hadn't been his fault, and Sam had always liked the rowdy bay colt.

It hadn't been hard persuading Brynna and Dr. Scott, the young vet on retainer to the Bureau of Land Management, to rescue the colt. The last time Sam had talked with Dr. Scott, though, he'd been worried over the colt's future.

"Are you putting him up for adoption?" Sam asked.

"Not yet. Dr. Scott wants to foster him out."

*Perfect*, Sam thought. That way the colt could get the loving care he needed.

Sam bolted to her feet and her gaze took in the ranch yard.

Where could they put an injured yearling?

The ten-acre pasture would be risky, but the barn corral held Tempest, her own black foal. Dark Sunshine, the filly's mother, was fiercely protective. She'd see a young male intruder as a threat.

Sam could easily imagine Sunny attacking Pirate. Even though he was young and injured, Sunny wouldn't take a chance with her foal's safety.

Sweetheart, Gram's aged pinto mare, had a box stall and indoor pen too small to share.

"Not here," Brynna said, though Sam was still scheming.

"Then where?" Sam asked.

"We have volunteers closer to town," Brynna said. Her voice sounded doubtful as she added, "Still, summer's a tough time to get round-the-clock care. People go on vacation."

Sam's hands perched on her hips and she gave a disgusted sound. She'd skip vacation if she could change life for an injured young horse. It was hard to believe not everyone felt that way.

"What about Mrs. Allen?" Sam suggested their neighbor, the owner of Deerpath Ranch who'd turned acres of her property into a mustang sanctuary.

"That might work, but not just yet. If all goes well, he should be able to be released with her herd in about a week," Brynna said. "Until then, he needs care for his injuries—hands-on care, Dr. Scott thinks, if he's going to adapt to captivity."

"Then why can't he just stay with Dr. Scott?" Sam asked. Obviously, that was the best solution of all.

Young, blond, and serious behind his black-rimmed glasses, Glen Scott was the vet who'd saved the Phantom's life when the stallion had been drugged and abused by an unscrupulous rodeo contractor.

"Dr. Scott's already stayed home for two weeks, caring for the colt," Brynna said.

Sam stiffened in surprise. Because the vet specialized in large animals, he made lots of house calls—pasture and barn calls, too. Around here, a person with a sick sheep, for instance, didn't expect to load it into a trailer and drive it to the vet's office. Instead, the vet drove to the sheep.

"BLM has already put far more money into the colt than it can ever hope to get back from the adoption fee," Brynna said.

Sam shrugged. That was always true. The vet care, vaccinations, food, and freeze branding given to wild horses that were captured on public lands was more expensive than the fee charged to adopters.

"So?" Sam said.

"So, we're at the point where whoever takes him into foster care will have to do it for free. Usually we pay the caregiver's expenses."

Brynna paused and shifted the waistband of her jeans.

"I'm going now. I'll check on the colt, then stop by my office."

"But it's Saturday," Sam said.

"I'm hoping I've received the fax about the new HARP girls. I should have had it Thursday."

The new HARP girls would arrive at the Reno airport tomorrow afternoon. Brynna always liked to know something about the girls before they showed up with their suitcases and varied backgrounds, ready to move into the new bunkhouse on River Bend Ranch.

"I hope to get back by lunchtime," Brynna said. "I don't blame you if you don't want to go."

"I want to, just let me tell Gram I'm going." Sam brushed her hands off on her jeans.

Finishing this chore later, in the heat of the day, would be a lot less fun, and her river walk with Tempest would be delayed, but she wanted to see Pirate.

"Sam." Brynna touched her shoulder before she could hurry off.

Sam stopped. Then she really looked at Brynna. It wasn't her stepmother's flush or the weary slump of her shoulders that worried her.

Sam's hands curled into tight fists and she drew a deep breath.

"What aren't you telling me about the colt?" Sam blurted.

"Maybe nothing. Maybe Glen's just grown too close to his patient." Brynna forced a smile.

Sam waited.

Finally Brynna rushed on, "I haven't seen the colt since you have, but he may be completely unadopt-able. Sam, from what Glen tells me, the colt's not only disfigured—he's crazy."

## *Chapter Two* ∾

*T*he only noise in the white BLM truck came from the air conditioner. It labored to cool the desert heat before it huffed in on Brynna and Sam, but it didn't do a very good job.

Sam barely noticed.

Never before had she heard Brynna use the word *crazy* for an animal. By nature and education, Brynna searched out a cause for unusual behavior. Usually she attributed horses' problems to humans.

Brynna might declare a horse *damaged* by bad care.

She might say a creature was *unhealthy* because of harsh range conditions.

She might say a horse had turned *vicious* in self-defense.

But *crazy?* Sam stared out the truck's side window, amazed the word was in Brynna's vocabulary.

As they drew near the Gold Dust Ranch, Sam's eyes focused.

She thought she saw clouds, but then she lowered the window for a better view. It was too hot and dry for clouds to be mounding and billowing like whipped cream, like foam on the tops of waves, like—

"Smoke," Sam gasped. "There's a fire at Gold Dust—"

"It's a controlled burn," Brynna said.

Sam sat back in her seat and clasped her hands in her lap when she realized she'd been gripping the window frame and she'd been sniffing the morning air like a dog.

*Calm down, can't you?* Sam said to herself. Not every fire was destructive.

"Oh," she said when Brynna glanced over at her. "Your dad said Jed Kenworthy took the Deerpath fire as a wake-up call. Since Linc didn't plant his hay fields this year, they're overgrown with cheatgrass. That's pretty much like kindling just waiting for a match. So Jed applied to the volunteer fire department for controlled burn permits. The volunteer fire truck will be out there off and on all week. They'll set the fields on fire, one at a time, then stand by, keeping watch."

Sam nodded. If another fire started before winter,

it'd burn to the edge of the blackened fields, then go out because of a lack of fuel.

Suddenly, the smell was a cozy reminder of childhood. So many ranchers burned off the stubbled fields after harvest that it was a seasonal scent, reminding her of frosty mornings and Halloween.

The smoky smell had seemed threatening because Linc Slocum, as usual, was out of step with the other ranchers. He hadn't raised hay because he could afford to buy it. He hadn't thought of the danger of a field of cheatgrass, because he didn't depend on Gold Dust Ranch to feed his family or pay his bills. To him, ranching was just a hobby.

"Quit moping. We're almost there," Brynna said.

Sam was so surprised, she didn't protest that she was *thinking*, not moping.

"Really?" Sam said.

As they drove through a neighborhood on the outskirts of Darton, Sam noticed that though the yards were larger than most in San Francisco, there was nothing like the ten-acre pasture on River Bend Ranch. Where could Dr. Scott keep horses?

"Yep, Raintree Road." Brynna read a street sign and turned right. "This is it."

"Are you sure he keeps patients here?" Sam asked.

"Positive," Brynna said. "He told me his house sits on a double lot and qualifies for agricultural zoning by six square inches."

Sam joined in Brynna's amusement. Dr. Glen Scott was exactly the kind of guy who'd measure his lot that closely, on his hands and knees if necessary, to get what he deserved.

"He told me it's the only yellow house on the block," Brynna said.

And there it was. The wooden house faced the street. A low white fence surrounded its tiny front yard, but there were no animals there.

They drove down a long driveway and discovered that the backyard was totally different. A rooster crowed from a row of cages and Sam saw what she was pretty sure were rabbit hutches.

Near the back of the property, Sam spotted a small corral and run-in shed. She didn't see the colt, but a half-grown Holstein calf, randomly spotted with black and white, bawled a noisy greeting.

"Glen must have very tolerant neighbors," Brynna said.

Sam was about to agree, when Dr. Scott leaned out the back door and motioned them inside. Brynna parked and set the emergency brake, then they headed for the vet's back porch.

*Where's Pirate?* Sam wondered. She scanned the property, feeling as if miniature mice were gnawing her nerves. She was that worried.

She kept looking for the young mustang, staring back over her shoulder as they climbed the concrete stairs, until she reached the door.

When Sam entered the crowded kitchen, she was distracted by the three gray kittens streaking out of the room.

The smell of burned toast lingered from breakfast, but the round kitchen table was bare and smeared with moisture, as if Dr. Scott had cleaned it for their arrival. The counters were clean, too, and empty except for a cage. The creaking sound must be coming from the white rat running on its wheel.

Sam thought of a painting called *The Peaceful Kingdom*, or something like that. Dr. Scott's kitchen was filled with creatures that were natural enemies — kittens, a rat, and . . . She peered into a decorative iron cage and discovered that it held a green parrot.

The big bird clung to the cage bars with talons, tilting its head sideways to ask, "Wanna beer?"

Sam and Brynna both caught their breaths with surprise as Dr. Scott corrected the parrot.

"*Cheer*. Want a *cheer*?"

By his patient tone, Sam guessed Dr. Scott had responded to the bird's question hundreds of times.

"He belongs to Mrs. Prizzo," he explained.

"The pastor at Bethany Church?" Brynna asked.

"Yes," Dr. Scott said. "So you can see the problem. She's had him since she was a girl and suddenly, with no encouragement, he's added that phrase to his vocabulary. She thinks he must have picked it up from television. In any case, she loves the bird and called me because she can't seem to cure him of this one bad habit. So I offered to give it a try."

"Are you making any progress?" Brynna asked.

The parrot squawked, left the cage bars for his perch, and sidestepped as far away from them as he could. He muttered as he moved.

"Cheer," Dr. Scott corrected loudly, then looked at Sam and Brynna. "He thinks if he mumbles I won't notice."

"Who's this?" Sam asked, pointing at the white rat.

"Francis," Dr. Scott said. "He's recovering from surgery to remove a bump from his tail."

A moo floated from the pen outside.

"You sure have lots of animals," Sam said.

"They're just patients," Dr. Scott said firmly. "Which brings us to our problem."

"Our equine burn victim," Brynna said. "I've been concerned about him."

"Wanna beer?"

"Cheer!" Brynna and Dr. Scott corrected the bird together.

"It's time for the colt to go. Come take a look." Dr. Scott started for the door, pausing to add, "Don't let the kittens out. They're orphans and they'd have no clue what to do in the yard."

Sam left the house first. The bay colt must have heard the kitchen door open, because he took a cautious step outside the run-in shed.

Sam's heart beat faster. The colt was moving normally, legs swinging with wild grace as he lifted his haltered head to get a better view of the humans.

A startled snort said he'd identified them as strangers, then he ducked back into the shed.

*That's a good sign*, Sam thought. After two weeks with Dr. Scott, the mustang was at least curious about people. Hiding in the shed wasn't that bad. She'd seen the colt's sire throw himself against fence rails until he was injured and exhausted.

"I'll walk on ahead of you and put the salve on his burns," Dr. Scott said. "If you stop here, you'll get a better look at him. He'll come to me and he's beginning to understand leading, but he's still pretty wild."

Sam stood with Brynna as Dr. Scott approached the corral at a brisk walk.

"Here, baby," he said in a voice higher than his normal tone.

Moving with wary steps and alert ears, the colt came out to meet the vet.

"He's going to have great conformation," Brynna said.

Just now, the yearling colt looked gawky. His body had a long way to grow before catching up with his legs. He reminded Sam of Damon, a freshman boy she knew at school. His basketball teammates called him Damon the Destroyer, not just because of his ability to demoralize opposing teams but because the kid couldn't cross a classroom without bumping into desks or tripping over feet—sometimes his own.

Sam figured Damon was clumsy because he was

as tall as a man but weighed less than most boys. And though he must be bruised from stumbling a lot, Damon was smooth and nimble when he was dribbling down the court to score.

The colt probably had his full height, too. She'd bet he was close to fifteen hands high, a fine size for a mustang stallion.

Could trauma have suppressed his appetite? Sam noticed how his bones poked against his coat at the same time she noticed what a beautiful color he was.

"He's a pretty bay, isn't he?" Sam said to Brynna.

"Dr. Scott thinks so. When I talked to him on the phone I was trying to fill out paperwork, and for coat color, he actually wanted to put *red topaz*."

"That doesn't sound like something you'd say about 'just a patient,'" Sam said. "And he called him *baby*."

Brynna nodded, but she didn't comment on Dr. Scott's obvious affection for the colt; she just said, "We decided he was a paint."

"Hmm," Sam said, but she guessed he was, even though she didn't see any white except the roughly starfish-shaped spot over his eye.

"Look how quietly he's standing," Brynna said when even the vet's upraised arms didn't frighten the colt.

The young horse protested by tossing his head and flaring his nostrils when the vet stood on tiptoe to apply the ointment, but he didn't bolt or strike out.

His movements seemed almost playful, reminding Sam of the first time she'd seen him.

On Dad and Brynna's wedding day, she'd been tracking down the Phantom's herd, though she should have been home at River Bend, where Jake had been waiting to drive her to the church.

She'd lost track of time as she watched the colt lead a troop of young horses in splashing mock battles in the desert lake at War Drum Flats. Then the snarl of a motorcycle passing on the highway had spooked the herd into running.

That's when the colt had panicked.

Sam had let Ace run with the herd, but she wasn't prepared for the colt's sudden appearance beside them. Fear had interfered with the colt's swift run and he'd crashed into the galloping gelding.

Ace had tripped and Sam had fallen, but the herd had split around her. Even though she'd been scuffed and dusty, she'd been fine.

Because of his distinctive markings, Sam had recognized the colt within the Phantom's herd each time she'd seen him. Most recently, she'd seen him race after a younger colt, when Linc Slocum's hunting dogs threatened the mustangs. Just like a herd stallion, the yearling had tried to shield the roan filly from danger, even when one of the dogs had slashed a ribbon of bay hide from his off hind leg.

The eye-patched colt was always bold and a little foolhardy, so she'd nicknamed him Pirate.

"Let's try taking a few steps closer," Brynna said,

and Sam couldn't help but notice her stepmother's professional tone. Was Brynna weighing the colt's adoption prospects?

One step closer turned out to be too many.

"Nope," Brynna said. As the colt shied fearfully, Brynna's arm reached out to gently bar Sam from moving closer.

When Brynna sighed, Sam said, "That proves he's not blind in the eye near the burn. That's good."

"It is," Brynna said, but she didn't sound enthusiastic.

"*I* think he's doing great," Sam said, standing up for the young horse. "Two weeks ago, he was as wild as any horse in the Phantom's band. Now he's letting Dr. Scott touch his head. That's incredible progress."

"He's got some other issues," Brynna said. *Issued.* For some reason, the word grated on Sam's nerves.

"Dr. Scott told me that the smoke damaged the colt's lungs, that he might not be able to tolerate dust storms or icy winter weather." Sam looked at the young horse who'd taken charge of all the other colts. He might have led a herd of his own one day, but not now. His days of freedom were over.

"Captivity's better than dying on the range, isn't it?" she asked Brynna. "He's pretty and smart and—"

"He's not so pretty anymore, Sam," Brynna interrupted. "Look at him with your eyes instead of your memory."

Sam shook her head. "So what? He's half gentled already. Dr. Scott said he's almost learned to lead. Anyone who adopted him would be getting a bargain."

All at once, Sam heard the colt's breathing grow louder. He staggered as if his legs had gone weak. His flanks darkened with sudden sweat. His ribs heaved over the rapid breaths swelling his lungs.

"There," Brynna said, but not with satisfaction. It was more like this reaction was something she'd been dreading.

"What's wrong with him?" Sam asked.

As they watched, Dr. Scott backed away from the colt, but only as far as he had to move for safety.

"It's okay, baby," he murmured. "You're safe."

When the colt remained oblivious, as if he could neither hear nor see the vet, Dr. Scott retreated step by slow step, until he reached the gate. Then he unlatched it without looking behind him, and backed through it.

Wearily, the colt let his head hang as he panted. One hoof struck the dirt repeatedly.

Settling his black-rimmed glasses into place and passing a hand over his hair, Dr. Scott finally reached them.

"What's wrong with him?" Sam asked.

"He's exhibiting all the signs of a horse in serious hyperthermia," the vet said, frowning. "Lethargy, weakness, rapid breathing, and flared nostrils, but he doesn't run a temperature. I've checked. He's not really hyperthermic."

"Is he sick?" Sam asked, but Brynna's question was louder.

"How often does it happen?" Brynna asked.

"Sometimes three times a day, sometimes not at all. This wasn't a particularly bad episode. See?" Dr. Scott nodded at the pen.

The colt shook his ears and looked around, as if he'd just awakened. If his coat hadn't still been wet from nervous sweat, Sam thought it wouldn't have been that hard to convince herself she'd imagined the incident.

"He's even hungry," the vet said as the colt sniffed a wisp of hay. "I probably didn't have to leave the corral."

"What does he do when it *is* a bad episode?" Sam asked, though part of her didn't want to know.

Dr. Scott cleared his throat before answering.

"He rears, rolls his eyes, and bursts into full terror response as if some door in his memory has opened onto an inferno."

Dr. Scott shaded his eyes with one hand as he stared at the colt. He bit his lip and was silent for so long, Sam was unprepared when he went on.

"And then," Dr. Scott said, "he screams, as if he's still burning."

## Chapter Three ∾

$S$am closed her eyes, wishing she could shut out the awful images for the colt. She'd had nightmares after her fall and concussion, but the colt's flashbacks to the fire would be a hundred times worse.

"He's having bad dreams," Sam said, but Dr. Scott shook his head.

"Not exactly. That would be understandable," Dr. Scott said, "but generally speaking, at least in human terms, if you have nightmares while you're wide awake, we call them hallucinations."

"A horse hallucinating?" Brynna asked. Her arms opened and her hands turned palms up, in disbelief. "Is that possible?"

Dr. Scott pushed his black-rimmed glasses up his nose, clearly uncomfortable with the diagnosis. "I admit I'm no expert on horse psychosis, but can you think of another explanation for what you just saw? I've tried for two weeks, and I can't."

Brynna stood quietly. Sam could almost see her logical stepmother reviewing the colt's symptoms.

He'd breathed quickly and loudly.

He'd staggered on suddenly weak legs.

He'd broken into a heavy sweat.

"Sure," Brynna said, with a quick nod. "It's been awfully hot lately. The thermometer outside my office reached a hundred degrees yesterday. Since he's not in the best health to begin with, he could be reacting to the temperature."

Then, as if Brynna was worried the vet would think she'd overstepped her expertise, she added, "But that must have occurred to you already."

"Of course, and there's nothing I'd like better than to believe it. But wait until you see a full-blown attack," Dr. Scott said, folding his arms. "It goes way beyond heat sensitivity."

They all stared at the horse as if he could explain.

"What if—in his mind—he's sort of connecting the fire's heat with the temperature?" Sam gestured at the August air. "Maybe he's forgotten he'd been hot before that—I mean, mustangs can't spend much time thinking about the weather. He might remember, though, how hot he was in the fire."

"Maybe," Dr. Scott said, but Sam could tell he wasn't convinced.

Then she remembered Dark Sunshine, not as the buckskin mare was now, but as she'd been a year ago.

"She screamed," Sam said slowly.

"He," Dr. Scott corrected before Sam could finish. "He's a stud colt, Sam."

"I know. I was thinking about Dark Sunshine," Sam told him. "When we first got her—"

"Stole her, to be accurate," Brynna said. She raised her eyebrows and gave a half smile, as if trying to lighten the mood. "Sam is quite an accomplished horse thief."

Sam didn't answer her stepmother's teasing. She was remembering Dark Sunshine's days with the owner who'd bought her from her adopter. The buckskin mare had been abused and used as bait in traps for other mustangs. Each time she'd felt the safety of a herd surrounding her once more, the other horses had been taken away and sold, and she'd been left behind.

It had been the mare's haunting screams, echoing from Lost Canyon, that had led Sam and her best friend, Jen, to investigate. Eventually she'd learned that Dark Sunshine's screams had started out as cries of loneliness, but they'd recurred whenever she was afraid.

Only kind, consistent care had cured the mare. Sam hadn't heard those awful neighs for months.

Crossing her fingers, she hoped she never would again.

"Why couldn't horses get freaked out by bad memories?" she asked the vet. "People do, don't they?"

"I'm not saying they can't," Dr. Scott's tone hardened. "What I am saying is, this colt needs to move on."

*That's not fair,* Sam thought.

Here, the colt had medical attention, company, and affection. How could there be a better place for him to recover? Sure it was rude to point this all out to Dr. Scott, Sam thought as she watched the injured colt sniff along the calf's furry back. But who else would speak for the young mustang?

As she was trying to compose words that would really work, Sam stared at the vet with such intensity, he looked away.

"I know what you're thinking," Brynna said, trying to head off Sam's argument.

"So do I," Dr. Scott said. "You think the colt belongs here. Thanks for the vote of confidence. Knowing how you feel about mustangs, I value that, but the timing's all wrong. What this colt needs now is daily, hands-on care."

Both Brynna and Dr. Scott had just assumed they could read her mind. And they were right.

"But you're giving him that kind of care," Sam said.

"Sam," Brynna cautioned. "A vet can't fall in love with all of his patients."

Dr. Scott gave a short laugh. "Even if I could, pretty soon I'd run out of money."

*Money. Why did it always have to be money?* Sam wondered.

"We've just about reached the limit of what BLM says I can spend on this colt," Brynna said. A worried frown creased her forehead.

"It's not that. I'll continue to treat him for free," Dr. Scott said. "But what about my other patients — the horses, cows, sheep, pigs, and dogs I drive to see around here?"

Frustration tightened Sam's chest. River Bend's animals had all benefited from Dr. Scott's care. What if he'd refused to come when they needed him?

"That colt's reached a critical period in his recovery," Dr. Scott said. "He's almost well. I've given him all the vaccinations and vitamins he needs and I'm tapering off his antibiotics. I think danger of infection is passed, as long as I —" He broke off with a shake of his head. "No. As long as his *new* owner applies his ointment."

"Is he healthy enough to be adopted?" Brynna asked.

"Physically? Sure, he's fine. He's learned to accept my touch, so other human hands shouldn't terrify him. As I said, this is the best time for him to bond."

"Except that he's *loco*," Sam said. Both Brynna and Dr. Scott stared at her in surprise. Since this did not sound like something she'd say, Sam explained,

"That's how Dad, Jed Kenworthy, or most ranchers would think, right?"

"Yep," the young vet agreed, but he met Brynna's eyes instead of Sam's.

What kind of plan had they worked out for the colt? They must have thought of something.

"Can't we take him to River Bend?" Sam asked.

"Honey, if we didn't have the HARP girls coming tomorrow, I'd probably face off with Wyatt and give it my best shot," Brynna said. "But we budgeted for last week's girls and they didn't come. That's nobody's fault, but we need this week's payment from HARP, and I don't think this colt would get the attention he needs while the girls are with us."

Sam drew a breath so deep, the hot air made her sneeze. Then she sighed. Brynna was right.

She looked back at the colt, studying his ugly burns. He needed every advantage he could be given. Someone should eat, sleep, and work near him. If he learned humans could make up his new herd, he'd not only be more adoptable, he'd be happier.

"Okay," Sam said as her mind sorted possibilities. Gold Dust Ranch? The Slocums had plenty of space and money. Jen would do a wonderful job working with the colt. For a minute Sam's spirits skyrocketed. Then they crashed. Jed Kenworthy wouldn't let Jen work with an injured mustang, for free, if she could be using the same hours to earn money helping HARP.

Besides, Sam scolded herself, Linc Slocum had almost destroyed Shy Boots, just because the foal wasn't a purebred. Her heart froze at the thought of how he'd treat a singed and psychotic mustang.

"What about Mrs. Allen?" Sam said.

The first fourteen horses sheltered at Blind Faith Mustang Sanctuary had been just like this colt—wild and unadoptable.

"She'd be first on my list," Brynna said.

Of course she would, Sam thought. Not only had Mrs. Allen successfully gentled Faith, a blind Medicine Hat pinto filly, to lead and accept humans; but Roman, the liver chestnut gelding who considered himself the boss of the captive mustangs, had been gentled to ride and very nearly won an endurance race.

Both had been slated for euthanasia because they were unadoptable, but both had healed under Mrs. Allen's care.

"She's all alone out there where it's quiet," the vet said. "She has plenty of time to pamper him, and some real expertise with horses."

"She'll do it," Sam said confidently. "I know she will."

Already Sam could picture the bright bay colt sharing the big square corral with Calico, Ginger, and Judge. The two paints and the old bay would be his new herd, crowding close to give him the security he missed.

"And she can put him in with her saddle horses," Sam said.

Dr. Scott was smiling, as if she'd guessed the right answer. "That'd be better than putting him out in the open pasture with the other mustangs," he added.

Better, too, Sam thought, because the wide pastures bordered the Phantom's territory. Running with a captive herd, with his home herd just outside the fence rails, would be too tantalizing.

"We've got the Willow Springs auction coming up soon," Brynna said. "And I make a point of telling a little about each horse. If I could mention he'd been handled for three weeks, if we could get him broken to lead by then . . ."

Brynna's words were hopeful, but her eyes weren't. A new owner would have to overlook the colt's damaged face and mind. Still, Brynna was willing to give it a try.

Sweat found its way from Sam's forehead to her right eyebrow. Then suddenly it sizzled in her eye.

*Stupid heat,* she thought. She loved summer, but about one week each year, she caught herself thinking no one with a brain had settled in northern Nevada during the hottest week of summer.

Sure, the early pioneers had stopped to plant trees and build cabins in springtime or fall. They might even have sheltered in the high desert in winter, since more days were cold and sunny than wet and dreary. But Sam knew if she'd been driving a covered wagon through northern Nevada during this August heat, she would have slapped the reins, clucked her tongue, and called out to her horses or oxen or whatever to keep on going.

The shade cast by the roof on the front porch of Brynna's office didn't seem to help much, and since the air conditioner in the beige government building had been turned off last night and no one had turned it on this morning, it was no better inside.

Sam longed for home, but Brynna wanted to talk with Mrs. Allen as soon as possible. Since Mrs. Allen's phone kept ringing busy, Brynna was alternately catching up on work and dialing.

If Sam had closed her eyes, she wouldn't have known she was looking out over hundreds of horses. A hoof stamped or a tail swished through the wind sometimes, but both were quiet sounds.

Willow Springs Wild Horse Center was a combination of what she loved and hated about the government's wild horse adoption program.

The pipe corrals help keep wild horses segregated by age and gender. They were a little more crowded than usual. Horses from holding corrals in other states were being sent to Willow Springs for the upcoming auction.

Of course, Sam was grateful that the horses had been rounded up and taken off the overgrazed range. In the old days, they might have been shot or captured and sold for pet food. Still, Sam hated it that none of the penned horses looked wild.

Sam pried a tiny rock from between two boards in the plank porch, turned it over on her palm, then threw it toward the dirt. After it struck the ground, Sam finally heard the flow of Brynna's voice from inside her office.

Sam couldn't tell what Brynna was saying, but she had to be talking with Mrs. Allen about adopting—or at least fostering—the burned colt.

Good!

The day was slipping away. Though she was eager to get the yearling's future settled, she could have finished weeding by now. She could have haltered Tempest and led her down to the river to wade. It wasn't likely Tempest would go without her mother, but the point of the walk was to continue accustoming the foal to her halter. When Sam pictured herself leading Dark Sunshine and Tempest, she saw herself wrapped in lead ropes, stumbling in all directions, trying to control both horses.

Suddenly the door opened behind her.

Smiling, Sam swiveled to look up at Brynna, then felt the muscles in her cheeks sag.

Before Brynna said a word, it was clear she felt dejected.

"She won't do it," Brynna said. Her shoulders sagged. The corners of her mouth drooped and Sam could see Brynna had counted on Mrs. Allen just as much as she had.

"Why?" Sam asked.

Looking resigned to Mrs. Allen's refusal, Brynna was about to go on, but Sam didn't give her a chance.

"That's why she has Blind Faith Sanctuary, isn't it? To shelter wild horses that have nowhere else to go?"

Sam felt angry, disappointed, and amazed, all at once.

"Sam, if you'd just listen—"

"What kind of excuse could she have? She could take him in for just a few days . . ."

Brynna's expression had changed. Her eyebrows arched, one higher than the other.

Sam's lips slammed closed. She had a feeling her stepmother was about to tell her she was being bratty beyond words. Or that she was babbling down the wrong track. Maybe both.

"I happen to think Mrs. Allen has a pretty good excuse," Brynna said quietly.

*Uh-oh.* Sam felt a hot blush clamp her face.

"She's picking up her grandson Gabriel at the airport tonight," Brynna continued, "and his doctors in Denver think Mrs. Allen's plans for this week could make the difference between Gabriel walking again, or staying in a wheelchair for life."

## Chapter Four

S am swallowed hard.

She'd talked with Gabe once. He'd been lying in a hospital bed, legs paralyzed by an accident that had happened a few days before the fire that had temporarily deafened the Phantom and burned Pirate. For some reason—maybe because Sam had been in an accident, too—Mrs. Allen had encouraged Gabe to call Sam.

She didn't remember much of the conversation, except that he'd made a dark joke. When she'd asked "What's up?", he'd answered "Not me."

She'd told him about the Phantom's deafness, too, and Gabe had told her he would let the stallion make up his own mind about returning to the wild. At the time, the suggestion had sounded insane. But that's just what Sam had done.

Maybe Gabe had an instinct for horses like she did. If only Mrs. Allen would accept the colt, Gabe might be able to help it recover. After all, they had a few things in common. The yearling had been a strong runner and a leader of other colts before the accident. Gabe was an athlete who'd made the varsity soccer team when he was only a freshman.

Sam's mind veered to school. With the beginning of classes just weeks away, Gabe had to be scared. Unless his condition had changed a lot, he might not be able to walk down the halls of his high school again, let alone play soccer.

"Taking care of her grandson's more important than the colt. Even I know that," Sam admitted. "But I can't believe they're letting him come here. When I got hurt, Dad sent me to San Francisco."

Two years ago, medical care in this part of Nevada had been hours away. Any complications could have killed her.

"He's told me how awful that was," Brynna said.

*Awful?* Dad sure hadn't acted like he felt that way. Sam remembered begging to stay home. Dad had refused, looking harsh and stubborn.

"First he lost Louise. Then he had to be separated from you. He told me"—Brynna paused and her voice softened—"that 'til then, he hadn't known a heart could break twice. But the doctors told him head injuries were risky, and you'd be safer in San Francisco, where you were minutes away from a hospital, instead of hours."

Sam didn't know what to say. She couldn't imagine Dad saying his heart had broken twice. And yet, he must have.

Brynna filled the silence with a sigh.

"So, thinking of that," Sam said, "aren't you kind of surprised they'd let Gabriel come here? I know things are better now, with the Angel Flight helicopter and stuff, but Mrs. Allen's ranch is even farther from town than River Bend."

Brynna shrugged. "Apparently the doctors agreed. I don't know the details, but Trudy said she'd promised him a trip out here before school started, and he wasn't about to let her back down from their deal."

*Wait a minute,* Sam thought. If the deal was the one she knew about and they still planned to go along with it, they were all crazy.

When Gabe had lain unconscious in the hospital, Mrs. Allen had flown to Denver to be with him. Sam had filled in as house, dog, and horse sitter and Mrs. Allen had called to check on things. Then, she'd told Sam she wanted to get Gabe up on a horse this summer, "no matter what."

Later, Mrs. Allen had amended that statement by saying they had plenty of time to teach Gabe to ride. Could he be holding his grandmother to her earlier promise?

Maybe, she thought, but why would his doctors go along?

"Has his condition improved a whole lot?" Sam asked.

"I don't know anything," Brynna said. She fanned herself with a couple of sheets of paper, probably the fax from HARP. "Except that we'd better get home and have some lunch before I faint."

Instantly Sam's knees straightened. She stood and her arms reached out to steady Brynna.

"Get off me," Brynna said, half laughing as she shrugged out of Sam's grip. "It's too hot for hugs."

"I'm not hugging you," Sam snapped, embarrassed as she realized that Brynna had been exaggerating, like everyone did.

She'd imagined Brynna pitching off the porch, face first to the ground, hurting herself and the baby she carried.

"Why did you say that? My heart is pounding like . . ."

Sam guessed Brynna must have seen past her rudeness to her concern, because she gave a sympathetic smile. "Sorry. It's just a figure of speech. I'm fine, just extra hungry since I'm eating for two."

Sam smiled as Brynna meant her to, but she didn't stop thinking of Pirate all the way home.

Lunch was finished. Sam, Dad, and Gram were still sitting at the kitchen table in the breeze from the ceiling fan, putting off the time when they'd have to continue their outside work.

Just as Sam began thinking of her walk with Tempest, the telephone rang. Brynna jumped up to answer it.

Refreshed and refueled, Brynna shifted from foot to foot, her eyes on Sam as she listened.

*It must be Jen*, Sam thought. Her best friend was almost psychic about trouble, especially horse trouble. Maybe she'd have a strategy for helping Pirate.

For the hundredth time, Sam wished their house had a telephone extension in another room. What she wanted to discuss with Jen was no secret; still, she'd enjoy a little privacy.

Lots of her school friends carried cell phones, but they weren't much of a solution. Cell coverage in this part of the high desert was spotty. Brynna joked that her government-issued cell phone was mostly good as a paperweight, and really a little light for that.

"Whoever's called isn't giving Brynna a chance to get a word in edgewise," Gram said, sipping the last of her iced tea.

That would be totally unlike Jen, Sam thought.

"Of course Wyatt wouldn't mind if you put your heads together," Brynna said.

Sam glanced toward Dad. He gave a grunt as if he weren't so sure he liked anyone, even his wife, speaking for him. Then Brynna said, "Sam, it's Mrs. Allen."

Brynna extended the phone and Sam scrambled up from her chair. It tipped and Sam barely caught it before it fell over.

"Careful," Gram cautioned.

"Sorry," she apologized, but her mind was already on the phone.

*Please let Mrs. Allen have changed her mind*, she begged silently.

"Hello?"

"Oh, Samantha, I can hear the hope in your voice, and I'm not at all sure I can help, but I'll try. I've been feeling awful since Brynna called." Mrs. Allen paused and tsked her tongue. "That poor burned little colt."

"If you could have seen him before . . ." Sam said, but her voice caught.

So few people had seen him whole and healthy. Born in the secret valley, he'd learned to run on broad white alkali flats that humans avoided. He'd hardened his hooves by climbing red rock plateaus that were a test even to mustangs.

Sam felt lucky to have seen the colt before the fire had scarred him forever. No one who saw him now would know how he'd been before.

"I've been thinking, Sam, if I took that colt in—"

"Oh, Mrs. Allen!" Sam rejoiced.

"—someone would need to take care of him, and by that I do not mean you, because I know how busy you are with the HARP girls and that darling black filly, but what about your friend Jen?"

When Sam didn't answer right away, Mrs. Allen said, "But Jen helps with the HARP girls, too, doesn't she?"

"She does," Sam said, but her mind sorted through every young rider she knew. Who could help? Someone had to.

"What about Callie, the girl who stayed with you here before?" Mrs. Allen suggested.

"She'd be perfect," Sam said.

Callie's gentle, otherworldly approach to horses charmed them. There was no other word for it. But Callie couldn't help either.

"She's decided to go back to school and she's applying for financial aid to pay for college classes. She says it's a full-time job filling out forms and sending them in."

"Oh, that's a shame," Mrs. Allen said. "I'd ask her to try to work it in anyway, but she doesn't exactly live nearby. . ." Sam's voice trailed off. She glanced at the kitchen table. Dad, Brynna, and Gram were still sitting there. They listened openly, but no one offered a suggestion.

"I'm afraid I just don't know many of the local teenagers," Mrs. Allen fussed.

"That's because there aren't many," Sam said. "Everyone lives in Darton except for me and Jen."

"Don't forget the Slocum twins," Mrs. Allen said grudgingly.

"There's no way Rachel—" Sam began.

"I've heard she's not the most responsible girl," Mrs. Allen said.

"She doesn't like horses," Sam said. "And Ryan is pretty busy with his own colt."

It was quiet for a minute. Sam swallowed, unsure why she didn't want to make the list of local teenagers complete. But then, she did.

"And there's the Ely brothers, of course."

"That's it!" Mrs. Allen's outburst made Sam hold the telephone away from her ear. "Jake Ely would be perfect. He has such a touch with horses, don't you think?"

"Yes, he does," Sam said. "But he'll be working with the HARP girls, too."

Jake could work wonders with the colt, but Jake was saving money for college, too. Would he be willing to take time out from his duties at Three Ponies Ranch and HARP work to help an injured mustang?

"But Jake would be perfect, Samantha," Mrs. Allen insisted. "Think about it. And he had the riding accident, too. I can't help thinking that another boy, a strong, athletic boy just like Gabriel, might be a help to him."

"I don't know," Sam said when she noticed Mrs. Allen's shift from the colt's welfare to that of her grandson. "Jake isn't the sympathetic type."

"How can you say that?" Mrs. Allen asked. "Why, that night my little Faith was lost in the snowstorm, he brought her home over the front of his saddle.

Samantha, you must remember. You gave me that lovely photograph."

In his leather coat and black Stetson, Jake had looked his tough, no-nonsense self as he carried the fragile, long-legged foal through the snow. Sam had to admit it was one of her favorites, too.

"I remember, but Jake's also the one who cut off his own cast before he was supposed to."

"Oh dear," Mrs. Allen said. "I wouldn't want him to encourage Gabriel to do anything other than what the doctors have ordered."

It was the perfect time to ask about Gabriel's progress, but Sam couldn't.

She wanted to know. She cared about the guy she'd talked with on the phone, late that night at Mrs. Allen's house, but her throat felt swollen shut. She could barely swallow and certainly couldn't form the words she needed to ask.

*He must be better or he wouldn't be coming here,* Sam told herself. And that was all she needed to know.

"I'm going upstairs for a nap." Voice lowered, Brynna tried to be quiet, but Sam glanced over to see Brynna kiss Dad's cheek and add, "Doesn't sound like I'll miss much."

Frustrated, Sam struck her thigh with her fist. There had to be a solution. Someone, somewhere must have the time to spend with the yearling.

"Maybe this is how things are supposed to work out," Mrs. Allen said.

"But who'll adopt him the way he is now?" Sam asked.

"Maybe no one," Mrs. Allen said. "Maybe the poor little fella wasn't meant to be tamed and adopted. It's unlikely he'll be put down with Brynna pulling for him, don't you think? Look at the bright side," Mrs. Allen said. "The BLM has those pastures out in the middle of the country. He could go to one of those."

For someone trying to be optimistic, Mrs. Allen's voice sounded forlorn.

"He's not the type to just graze his life away," Sam said. "That's not much better than just keeping him sedated, like Dr. Scott's been doing so far."

The rambunctious colt deserved better, Sam thought.

Gram shifted in her chair at the table, and Sam wondered why she looked so distressed. But Sam looked away when she heard Mrs. Allen take a troubled breath.

"I'll keep thinking," Sam said, trying to reassure her. "Mrs. Allen, you're doing all you can. Your grandson needs you more than the colt does. I know that."

"Thank you, dear," Mrs. Allen said. "You've been a great help over the past couple weeks and I appreciate it more than you know. I hope you'll get to be great friends with Gabriel while he's here this week. . . ."

*Great friends?* Sam definitely didn't see that happening. She might have time to ride over to Mrs. Allen's house once this week, or Gram might drive her over to visit, but "great friends" didn't happen in an hour or two.

". . . call me back when you work out a plan," Mrs. Allen concluded.

Sam blinked in surprise. *When* she worked out a plan? She appreciated Mrs. Allen's faith in her, but didn't she mean *if*?

**But this was no time to dump her own doubts on Mrs. Allen, so Sam promised, "I will."**

She hung up the phone and stood with her arms crossed, wondering what to do next.

"So she has her hands full with her grandson?" Gram asked.

"He's there for only a week," Sam explained. Of course it had to be the week before the auction. Would it really matter to Gabriel if he came to Deerpath Ranch a week later? It would matter to Pirate. A single week of gentling could give him an edge over the other mustangs up for adoption. He'd be sweeter and more likely to get a home.

**But Sam didn't say that. She knew it would sound pouty and insensitive, even though it was the truth.** Instead, she told Gram about Mrs. Allen's offer: She'd let the colt stay at her ranch, but someone else would have to care for him.

"Honey," Dad said.

Sam had almost forgotten Dad was still sitting at the kitchen table. But there he was, wearing a blue chambray shirt, long sleeved to protect him from the sun. He was drinking a cup of hot coffee, too, even though it was a million degrees outside.

"Yes?" Sam asked, hoping Dad could point a way out of this maze of confusion.

"We can do without you this week."

One drawback to having a cowboy father was that he spoke briefly, with no explanations or details.

"Do you mean Jen can take over?"

"And Jake," Dad said.

Okay, Sam thought. That made sense. There were only two HARP girls coming, so they wouldn't really need three teachers.

It would have been great if Dad had gone on for a few minutes about how it wouldn't be the same without her. Or if Gram had mentioned the girls would really miss out on a great teacher, but Sam knew that was unlikely.

She did a good job. They knew it. She knew it. So why waste words talking about it?

"So it's okay with you if I tell Mrs. Allen I'll come over and take care of the colt?" Sam asked.

Even though Jake or Callie would probably do a better job, Sam knew she should grab the opportunity. She might be Pirate's best hope.

So why did she feel like there was some snag in this smooth way out?

"I can't leave Tempest," Sam said suddenly.

"Well, you certainly can't take her with you," Gram said.

"I could," Sam said, trying to figure out how that would work.

"It's too early to wean her," Gram said. Her tone hinted that Sam should know better than to even suggest such a thing.

"I wouldn't wean her," Sam said. "I could take Dark Sunshine, too."

Dad gave a disgusted snort and pushed away from the table to stand.

"Don't ask me to be part of your travelin' circus," he said, sounding impatient.

Sam bit her lip.

Dark Sunshine was half wild under the best of conditions. In a strange place, she'd feel more protective of her foal, more hyperalert and wary. Pirate didn't need that kind of influence in the next corral. Okay, so taking Dark Sunshine and Tempest with her was a crazy idea. But she still felt torn.

"Well, it's not like I won't be handling her for a week. I just won't have as much time with her," Sam said. She slid her eyes sideways, watching Dad. In fact, she was testing him. And he knew it.

"Wrong. If you're going over to help with that burnt colt, you're staying there. A halfway job is worse than no job at all."

"You'd make me stay over there?" Sam asked.

"I'm not making you do anything," Dad said. He took his cowboy hat from the rack by the kitchen door. "Go or stay, Samantha. It don't make any difference to me."

*Chapter Five* ⌒

The door closed behind Dad.

Openmouthed, Sam turned toward Gram.

"He's just testy because of the heat," Gram assured her.

"I hope you're right," Sam said as she bolted out the kitchen door after him.

Her first step into the Nevada sun was as dazzling as it was hot. Shading her eyes against the glare, Sam sprinted to catch up with Dad.

He must have heard her steps pelting closer across the sandy ranch yard, because he turned and waited.

"What would *you* do?" Sam asked.

"Couldn't say," Dad told her. "But one week's not

worth wastin' a whole day thinking about it. Go, if you think you can do the colt some good. Stay, if you think home is where you need to be."

A high-pitched, fussy squeal interrupted them. It meant that Tempest had spotted Sam.

Sam glanced over to see the black filly peering through the fence around her pen. It hadn't taken long for Tempest to learn that Sam was the one person on River Bend Ranch who was guaranteed to pay attention to her.

*My baby is spoiled,* Sam thought, as a second, more demanding whinny floated to her.

"Sam," Dad said as his big hand closed over her shoulder and gave it a gentle shake. "You've hardly slept in your own bed this summer, but I'm proud of what you've done since school let out. Go try your hand with that colt, or stay and help the HARP girls. Either way, it's fine with us.

"Now, I've got to ride out and see how long I can leave that hay in the field."

Sam thought about last year's haying as Dad walked away. They'd come close to losing the entire crop because they'd waited until the last minute to harvest.

"It's the same sort of decision, isn't it?" Sam asked.

Dad stopped.

"What's that?" he asked, frowning.

"If you leave the hay out too short a time, it's

green and bad for the animals. If you leave it out too long, there's a risk of it being damaged by rain or frost."

Dad nodded as if he were following her so far.

"If I go help with the mustang, Tempest is without me, and . . ."

The rest of the comparison was a little harder to explain, and Dad had run out of patience.

Dad nodded. "It's a balancin' act, all right. Tell me at dinner what you decided."

The buckskin mare and black colt weren't going to help her decide, either, Sam thought as she climbed the corral fence to look inside.

Dark Sunshine stood in the gray shade of her corral fence. Fine-boned and nervous, she rarely looked so relaxed. With eyelids lowered, the buckskin held one back hoof cocked on its point. Her black-edged ears tilted out to each side. She looked half asleep as she stood beside Tempest.

Although the filly had been calling to Sam, beseeching her to play just minutes ago, Tempest was sprawled in the small patch of shade cast by her mother. She lay flat on the short grass, eyes closed, long legs extended as if even in her sleep, she was running.

Sam wished her life were so easy.

Why was it that anytime she wanted to make her own decision, her family refused to allow it? Then, when she wanted help and direction, they said she had to make her own choices?

She had to decide between Tempest and Pirate. She wanted to stay home during these last few weeks of summer and cement her bond with Tempest. And she wouldn't mind earning another paycheck from HARP. Soon, Gram would drive her to the Crane Crossing Mall for school shopping and Sam knew she'd want a few things Gram would call luxuries and refuse to buy.

But who would help Pirate if she didn't? And he *could* be helped. She felt sure of it.

At Dr. Scott's house, the damaged colt had trembled and panted, but he hadn't struck out at ghost flames. He might be scared, but she didn't think he was crazy.

Sam definitely didn't want to spend another week at Mrs. Allen's house. The lavender ranch house had only one spare bedroom and certainly it should be Gabriel's.

A hot breeze, as if someone had opened a huge oven door, blasted past Sam. Could you be so hot that you were cold? Sam didn't know, but a shiver prickled down her forearms.

It would be awkward to stay at Mrs. Allen's house, but what if one more week of kindness could soothe away Pirate's bad memories? What if she slept in a sleeping bag outside the corral, while Mrs. Allen's three old saddle horses—Calico, Ginger, and Judge—acted like a cozy family to the frightened yearling?

Dad had said he'd like to hear her decision at dinnertime, but Dr. Scott wanted the foal moved right away. According to Brynna, if Pirate didn't go to Deerpath Ranch, he'd go to the corrals at Willow Springs Wild Horse Center.

Sam fanned the hem of her tank top, cooling her tummy.

She'd make up her mind soon, but she'd think better if she weren't so hot, and that meant taking Tempest wading.

Instead of going inside the barn, walking through Dark Sunshine's box stall and out into the small pasture, Sam threw one leg over the top of the fence, then climbed down as if the rails were rungs on a ladder.

A low nicker told her Dark Sunshine noticed, but she only watched as Sam's tennis shoes touched the ground.

"Get up, lazybones," Sam called to Tempest. "Time to go down to the river."

The foal's long black legs thrashed. She scrambled upright, tiny hooves barely touching the ground before she ducked to the other side of her mother.

Sunny curved her neck and nuzzled the filly's withers, comforting her.

Reassured, Tempest lowered her head to look under Dark Sunshine's buckskin belly, then gave a snort.

"Yep, it's only me," Sam said. She made a smooching noise and held out her hand. Tempest looked back over her shoulder and gave three quick nods that made her fuzzy forelock bob, but she didn't stop. She followed her mother as the mare moved toward the barn.

A dusty haze surrounded the horses as Sam entered the box stall. It was a little risky, being in this confined space with the mare and foal, but Dark Sunshine knew what came next. The mare had learned to enter her stall, allow herself to be haltered and led.

"You're a good girl," Sam praised the mare, then slipped past her through the stall door, grabbed the halters, and returned.

The mare dropped her head and stood still for the halter to be buckled on.

"This is your passport out of here, isn't it, beauty?" Sam asked.

For a few weeks, Dark Sunshine had run wild with the Phantom. Her sturdy legs had galloped many miles, and sometimes she gazed toward the Calico Mountains with longing. But the mare was settling in. Shortly after Tempest's birth, she'd had a chance to leave with the Phantom, and she'd stayed home at River Bend Ranch, instead.

"If we ever get a saddle on you, we can go lots farther away," Sam told the mare as she picked a wisp of straw from her black mane. "Think of it, girl."

As she said the words, Sam realized lots of people—in fact, most people—would call her a nutcase for asking a horse to think about anything.

Luckily Pepper, Ross, and Dallas, the River Bend

cowboys, who definitely would have laughed, were out on the range, not eavesdropping outside the barn.

If Sunny considered the idea of carrying a saddle and rider, she didn't think much of it. She snorted and stiffened her legs.

"Say what you want," Sam told her. "But it would really speed up your baby's lessons if I could ride you and lead her."

Dark Sunshine tossed her head in what Sam guessed was the horse equivalent of a shrug. Then Sunny blew through her lips as if saying, "Whatever."

The mare watched carefully, though, as Sam prepared to halter Tempest.

Dad had hand-stitched the foal's soft leather halter and Sam had kept its brass rings and buckles polished bright.

Smelling milky and feeling warm from the sun, Tempest crowded Sam, so eager to put her muzzle in the noseband that she made it almost impossible.

"Hey, baby girl," Sam crooned, "give me a second."

Once she had the noseband in place, Sam lifted the cheek pieces up, laid the thin strap behind the filly's satiny black ears, and threaded it through the buckle.

As soon as the buckle was fastened, Tempest butted her forehead against Sam's chest.

"I'm hurrying," Sam said. Though she'd been braced for it, the filly had given her a pretty good thump. "Don't be bratty," Sam teased.

Their ritual called for Sam's fingers to finish buckling, then rub the always-itchy spot behind Tempest's ears.

The ranch yard lay still before them. Even the hens had taken shelter from the heat inside their coop, but the horses surged against their lead ropes, nostrils flared to catch scents from the river. A few yards behind the horses, Blaze tagged along, panting. The temperature couldn't have dropped more than a couple of degrees as they neared the river, but relief blew toward Sam when she smelled the scents of water, vegetation, and hot rocks.

Sunny gave a low, contented neigh. Tempest tried to lift her knees in a half rear and kick out with her hind hooves at the same time, and Sam held on to their lead ropes, hoping for the best.

This was the first time she'd tried tying the buck-skin to anything besides the hitching rail, and Sam was a little scared. If the mare felt restricted or con-fined, she might start bucking. That could be danger-ous for all three of them.

"Okay, Sunny, I'm gonna loop this rope around this cottonwood tree," Sam said when they reached the edge of the river. "And I'm going to try to—Blaze, no barking!"

Amused by Sam's contortions as she gripped Tempest's lead rope with one hand and tried to tie a square knot with the other, the Border collie bowed his head between widespread front paws, waved his tail, and gave a yodeling growl.

"Real funny," Sam muttered. Then, as if Blaze had given her instructions on how to tease Sam further, Tempest walked steadily toward the river. "We'll go wading in a minute," Sam promised, but the filly didn't understand.

Sam gasped as her arms were pulled in opposite directions.

"Please stop," she begged, but she didn't dare yank the lead rope.

The filly's halter-breaking had progressed really well, but one rough experience could be a setback.

After another bark, Blaze sat. His tongue lolled and his eyes gleamed as if he were enjoying a joke, but his silence made Tempest stop and glance at her mother.

Sam sighed. "Thanks, baby," she said to the filly. "I thought you were going to split me in two."

Despite the turmoil, Dark Sunshine stood quietly as Sam tightened the knot, then stepped back with Tempest to watch.

Sunny stared over the La Charla to the wild side of the river.

Did the mare see or hear mustangs? Sam's heart beat more quickly.

"What is it, Sunny?" Sam asked, but the mare only shivered the skin on her neck, twitching away invisible pests.

Maybe it gave her chills, looking to the Calico Mountains and knowing the Phantom was up there somewhere. Sam knew just how the mare felt.

*Back to work,* Sam told herself. Then, with Sunny looking on, she held the end of Tempest's lead rope and followed the filly to the water's edge. Tempest looked down. She stared past the silver ripples, through the shallow water to the sandy river bottom. She stamped one hoof, then gave a little buck at the sudden shower.

"Just like your sire," Sam told her.

The Phantom had started playing in the water as a young black colt, and he'd never stopped. Each time Sam had seen him at the La Charla, he'd managed to drench them both by splashing in the river water.

As the filly delighted in making her own rainstorm, Sam wrapped the lead rope several times around her right hand, gripped it hard, and concentrated on toeing off her tennis shoes.

Barefooted, she waded in, spotted a patch of river bottom without many rocks, and began Tempest's lesson.

She pulled the rope gently to one side, then the other. She held her breath, but she didn't have to wait long for the filly to step forward.

"Good girl!" Sam said. "You are the best!"

Tempest's head bobbed, agreeing. Sam wanted to wrap her arms around the filly's velvety neck.

Instead, she remembered how Sunny had nuzzled Tempest's withers to reassure her. Sam rubbed Tempest's withers with her fingers to see if she could do it, too.

When the filly relaxed and yawned, Sam decided she'd added to her equine vocabulary. Not only that, she knew she had to spend the last few weeks of summer with Tempest.

Someone else would have to help Pirate.

The thought hurt. She felt as if a bone had cracked in her chest, but she knew it was only guilt.

She rubbed Tempest's withers and told herself someone would feel sorry for the colt and adopt him. But is that what that strong colt, who'd once run wild and free, deserved?

Tempest's peaceful moment didn't last long. A quiver ran over her as Dark Sunshine gave a snort.

Sam followed the filly's eyes and saw Dark Sunshine tighten up. In an instant, she looked more like a seventeen-hand horse than one that barely measured fourteen hands.

The mare had spotted Dr. Scott's truck. Judging from the way her ears flattened, she hadn't forgotten the shots and examinations she'd hated during her pregnancy.

"Give him a break, Sunny," Sam said. "He loves animals, even you."

Then Sam noticed that Blaze was slinking away, headed toward the brush beside the river.

"Blaze, come back here!"

The Border collie glanced over his shoulder at her. His black face, bisected by a white hourglass shape, looked sheepish and apologetic, but he kept going.

The young vet parked and climbed out of his truck. If he noticed Blaze's disappearance or Sunny's glare, he didn't show it.

Dr. Scott's jeans were smeared with dirt. His blue-and-white-checked shirt was so rumpled that Sam suspected he'd pulled it out from under his bed that morning. Still, he looked happy and excited.

"Brynna tells me Mrs. Allen said *no problema* about the colt staying at her place this week."

Sam didn't pay as much attention to the vet's fractured Spanish as she did the content. Had Brynna skipped right over that whole midmorning panic? The part where Mrs. Allen had said "no"?

"Yeah, but she can't work with him," Sam hinted.

"Right, something about her grandson's accident," Dr. Scott said distractedly.

"Her grandson's *really serious* accident," Sam repeated, with the emphasis she thought it deserved.

Then she noticed Dr. Scott's eyes. Behind his black-framed glasses, the vet focused on Blaze. The dog was wandering back from the river. Once he saw Dr. Scott watching, Blaze lowered his head and stopped. His plumy tail nearly touched the ground as it waved a cautious greeting.

The vet glanced at Sam, raised his eyebrows, then purposely turned his back to the dog so it could approach unwatched.

Then, arms folded over his belt, Dr. Scott faced Sam.

"Is anything wrong?" Sam asked suddenly. She looked quickly toward the bridge that led to River Bend.

"No, I'm just driving over to Deerpath Ranch to see what kind of setup Mrs. Allen has for the colt. Thought I'd stop on my way and tell you about my observations this morning."

Why couldn't she find the words to tell him that she wasn't going to take care of Pirate? If she did, he might change his mind about evicting the colt from his corral.

Then Sam wondered if she'd come up with a crack in the vet's emotional armor.

*The colt.* Dr. Scott never called him anything else. If *she'd* been caring for a young horse for two weeks, she certainly would have named it. Maybe he had, and just wouldn't admit it.

"What's the colt's name?" she asked, as if she could catch him off guard.

"He doesn't have a name, Samantha," Dr. Scott said patiently. "He's a wild horse."

Dr. Scott's tone—which implied she wasn't too smart—would have been insulting if she hadn't known he was underlining the fact, again, that he didn't get involved with his patients.

Sam thought about telling him that she called the colt Pirate, but something stopped her.

"At any rate," Dr. Scott went on, "this morning, I was out putting on his salve and sunscreen—"

"Sunscreen?"

"I'll tell you all about it when we meet at Blind Faith tomorrow morning."

"But, I'm not sure I'm going—"

Blaze interrupted Sam's confession by sidling next to the vet. Then the Border collie raised his head under Dr. Scott's hand, forcing a pat.

Sam looked at the vet, incredulously, but the surprises weren't over.

With a low nicker, Dark Sunshine nudged the small of the vet's back. He turned and rubbed her neck.

"What happened, do you think?" Sam asked.

"I know exactly what happened," Dr. Scott said. "They noticed I wasn't carrying my bag—the one with the shots and medicines in it."

"Of course," Sam said. The animals were more observant than she was.

"Yeah," he said pointedly, "it turns out, a lot of times, it's kinda hard to recognize what's good for you."

Sam had a feeling he wasn't just talking about the animals.

*Chapter Six* ❧

"**I** really need to put some time in with Tempest before school starts," Sam insisted.

"Just listen to what I have to say." The vet's calm voice made Tempest look up.

Drops of river water trembled on her black face as if someone had decorated her with rhinestones. The filly's beauty tugged at Sam's heart, but she nodded. She'd listen to Dr. Scott, but he wouldn't change her mind.

"First off, if you don't work with that injured colt, no one will. Not in time for the auction."

He was probably right, Sam thought.

"Second, I'm not just asking you to do this for the good of the colt, but for your own good, too. I know that's a parent kind of thing to say, and I grant you, helping that little paint will be a lot harder than what you're doing with this baby."

Together they looked at Tempest. Without thinking, Sam touched the cheek that was still faintly marked where Tempest's hoof had cut her on the first day of halter-breaking.

Dr. Scott must have followed her thoughts, because he gave a dismissive wave.

"With the wild colt, there's a greater chance of failing than there is of success. . . ."

"Great." Sam hadn't meant to say it. The word had just popped out.

"But you'll change his life if you work with him. Tempest will be waiting for you when you're done."

"I appreciate what you're saying—" Sam started, but Dr. Scott wasn't finished.

"I don't have to tell you there are better riders than you," he said.

"No," Sam put in. Why did he think that would be persuasive?

"But you have an instinct for thinking like a horse that is, in my experience, unparalleled."

Sam took a deep breath, thinking about the compliment. She pictured two twigs lying side by side. Parallel to each other, right? Then she imagined railroad tracks running into the distance, with only one rail on the right side and the crosspiece meeting nothing on the left.

Unparalleled. It was difficult to believe Dr. Scott, but if he happened to be right, maybe the injured colt could complete the picture. Maybe Pirate could be the other rail running along beside her. What if she *could* help him, and he transformed into as wonderful a tamed horse as he had been a wild one?

Sam shook her head. It just didn't make sense. Jake could do that, but her?

"What if I'm not good enough?" Sam asked. "What if I just scare him even more?"

"So, you think it's better not to try?"

"No. Of course not, but what if I try and—"

"Sam, if you try hard enough, you'll improve his life, forever."


Sam wished she'd worn her bathing suit to bed.

According to the thermometer outside the kitchen, it had still been eighty-two degrees when she'd gone upstairs.

"Take a glass of ice water up with you and just try to sleep," Gram had urged her.

That had been at about ten o'clock, but she'd just heard the grandfather clock strike one.

She would have stroked Cougar and let his purr lull her to sleep, but the last time she'd seen her cat, he'd been stretched out in front of the kitchen's screen door, hoping for a breeze.

It was ridiculous, lying flat on her back with her arms out so they didn't touch her nightgown. She'd need her sleep to be ready for tomorrow, but that thought made her mind swirl faster.

Dr. Scott's praise had convinced her to help Pirate.

For her, it had been a big decision, but when she'd told Dad, Brynna, and Gram, they'd just nodded their agreement, then ignored her as they prepared for the HARP girls' arrival.

Brynna had been on the phone, talking with Mrs. Allen, for nearly half an hour. Since Brynna had to drive into the Reno airport to pick up the HARP girls and Mrs. Allen had to make the same trip to meet Gabe's plane, the two women had tried to consolidate the trips into one.

From what Sam heard, it wouldn't work, but she'd been more concerned about the time she'd spend with Mrs. Allen and Gabe once he was at his grandmother's ranch.

"I'm not sure how I'm supposed to act around Gabe and everything," Sam had told Dad.

He'd nodded slowly and for a minute, she'd thought he understood her worries, but then he'd tousled her hair and said, "I'll get you over to Deerpath nice and early, don't you worry. I'm sup- posed to pick up that new truck you won for me by nine."

Getting there early wasn't the point at all, but she'd just smiled and hoped she'd figure out how to handle the awkward situation when she got there.

She'd packed some clothes. They weren't the ones she wanted, but Gram had said any laundry Sam washed would have to go with her wet, because there was no way on earth they'd run the dryer and make the house even hotter.

"If you didn't throw your clothes on the floor after you've worn them once, you wouldn't have this problem," Gram had muttered, but then she'd looked up from her weeklong menu with a sigh. "I don't mean to sound snappish, honey. One of the HARP girls is allergic to eggs and I'm trying to figure out how I will adapt."

"That's okay, Gram," she'd said, but when she'd tried to talk with Brynna about how Pirate would be handled during the wild horse auction, her stepmother had been busy going over the juvenile records and personal histories of the girls.

Finally, a breeze ruffled the curtains at Sam's window. Faint but cool, it reached her and she sighed. Paws padded into her room and Cougar leaped onto her bed.

Sam's bedsprings creaked as she rolled over to see Cougar kneading her sheets into a suitable nest. The cat was as particular as she had been, digging her sleeping bag out of a downstairs closet, shaking it out, and rerolling it into a smooth bundle, tied tight until she unfurled it tomorrow night at Mrs. Allen's ranch.

"Go to sleep," Sam urged the cat. Cougar pretended not to understand.

She knew she wouldn't be sleeping at home tomorrow night, but Pirate didn't. He'd found a home off the range in Dr. Scott's corral, but he was about to lose it.

Sam swallowed hard. She had to help the colt through his pain and confusion. If she succeeded, he could be adopted into a loving home. If she failed, he'd live out his days in a faraway pasture. One way or another, he'd be gone soon.

At last, Cougar gave a feline sigh. Without meaning to, Sam echoed it.

The cat lay still and so did Sam, fading into dreams of sun glare, galloping hooves, and the river, shushing her worries into silence.

The next morning, Sam was kissing Ace good-bye on his velvety muzzle when Dad told her to hop in the car.

Deerpath Ranch was only a few miles out of the way, so Dad and Gram were dropping Sam off before starting toward Darton to pick up Dad's new truck. Sam sat in the backseat of Gram's yellow Buick, arms wrapped around her sleeping bag.

Gram glanced over her shoulder.

"You've stayed there before," Gram said.

"I know," Sam said.

*But not without my horse,* she thought. Both times she'd stayed at Deerpath Ranch—first helping the blind filly Faith through her first rocky days, then when Mrs. Allen had flown to Denver after Gabriel's accident—Sam had brought Ace along with her. But Sam was pretty sure Gram wouldn't understand that the frisky bay gelding could be her security blanket.

*Boo hoo, poor you,* Sam scolded herself. How many girls would love the chance to spend a week on a ranch, sleeping out under the Western stars, working to heal a wild mustang?

Hundreds, maybe thousands of people would envy her.

By the time they reached Deerpath Ranch, Sam barely noticed the improvements Mrs. Allen had made to the ranch this past year. Wooden fences had replaced rusted, sagging barbed wire. Bleached and barren fields had become green pastures, spreading to the horizon, dotted with glossy-coated mustangs.

Sam couldn't wait to get started. She opened the car door and shoved out her sleeping bag and suitcase.

A neigh floated to her from the barn corral.

Two pintos and a bay watched her, tails swishing, heads tossing. Calico, Ginger, and Judge didn't know they were about to get a new roommate.

No tangerine-colored truck sat parked by the wrought-iron fence around the rose garden, so Mrs. Allen hadn't come home yet. Dr. Scott's truck and trailer weren't here, either.

Sam climbed out after her stuff, and slammed the door.

Gram opened her door, went to the Buick's trunk, and opened it to remove a Styrofoam cooler. Sam had seen her put in plastic containers that held casseroles, cinnamon rolls, and vegetables all cut up and ready to dunk in the *chili con queso* dip.

"This might give her a few extra hours to spend with Gabriel, instead of cooking," Gram said, but they both knew Mrs. Allen didn't cook much. "And don't forget these."

Gram lifted out a brown paper bag. Sam could smell the yeasty aroma of fresh bread, wrapped and sitting atop tomatoes and zucchini from Gram's garden.

"I guess we beat everyone," Sam said.

Gram scanned the deserted ranch, then looked back at Dad. "Wyatt?"

Sam knew she was to blame for Gram's hesitance. "I'll be fine," she assured Gram. "I'll just go yell through the door so that Imp and Angel know it's me." She smiled, knowing Dad and Gram could hear Mrs. Allen's dogs barking with as much ferocity as their twenty-pound bodies could manage. "Then I'll go climb up in the tree house. I'll know even before they do if someone's coming."

"Fine," Dad said, but he motioned Sam to the driver's side window.

"Remember you were talkin' last night about Gabriel?" Dad paused until Sam nodded. "Just treat him like you'd want to be treated if you switched places. Don't go lookin' for trouble. Just do your best and that'll be plenty good enough."

Coming from Dad, that was a huge lecture. Sam leaned down to kiss his tanned and weathered cheek.

"Meant to ask you," he added as she pulled away, "you leave your hat home on purpose?"

Sam smoothed her hand from her crown to the auburn hair covering the nape of her neck. It already felt hot with morning sun.

"I did," she said. "Dr. Scott never wears one, and since he's the only human the colt really knows . . ."

Gram leaned forward and stared across Dad at Sam.

"That is awfully good thinking," Gram said.

"Yep," Dad agreed.

"I know you'll do right by that young horse."

"Thanks, Gram," she said.

Sam was still smiling as she stared after Gram's yellow Buick. Bumping down the road, it left her alone at Deerpath Ranch.

The black iron gate squawked. Metal shouldn't make a sound like that, Sam thought as she approached Mrs. Allen's house. Maybe the hinges needed oil or something.

The squawk set off a chorus of barks from inside the house. Sam eased through the gate and started up the garden path to Mrs. Allen's lavender house.

Sam knew the twisted metal spikes on the fence

were just for decoration. They probably weren't sharp, but she remembered walking up this garden path hand-in-hand with Jake when they were six or seven years old, thinking Mrs. Allen was a witch.

Sam didn't feel that way anymore, and once she got past the iron gate, the garden surrounding her was crowded with lush flowers and the buzz of honeybees.

She didn't expect anyone to answer her knock, but Imp and Angel did their best, barking and bouncing against the front door.

"It's just me, guys," Sam shouted.

Even though she'd bet Mrs. Allen hadn't locked her door, Sam didn't let the black-and-white Boston terriers out. She could imagine them tearing around like the devil dogs she'd once thought they were, terrifying Pirate or Gabe—whoever arrived first—before she could recapture them.

Because she didn't want Mrs. Allen to think she planned on sleeping in the house, Sam piled her gear by the corral. It would be great to bed down outside, near the horses. Even as he drowsed, the injured colt would catch her scent and know she meant him no harm. She was just part of his herd. At least, temporarily.

Sam strode away from the ranch yard toward the tree house that had been built for Mrs. Allen's children. It was weird to think that Gabriel's mother had probably sat up in this tree house, having picnics, maybe, or daydreaming she lived in the turret of a castle. She never could have guessed that some stranger named Samantha Forster would sit here, waiting to meet her injured son.

Except, that wasn't the main point, Sam thought a bit guiltily. She hoped Dr. Scott arrived first with the colt.

There was no sign of anyone yet.

From the tree house, Sam could see Mrs. Allen's house—gardens and studio in one direction and the blackened fields in the other. The La Charla River ran along one edge of the Blind Faith Mustang Sanctuary. Its other boundaries were marked by brown-red fences Sam had painted herself. To the east, she saw the stairstep mesas leading up to the Calico Mountains and felt her pulse speed up as if she'd begun sprinting toward them.

The Phantom's secret valley lay hidden in those mountains. The silver stallion roamed this territory more often than he did the range surrounding River Bend.

Sam crossed her fingers on both hands. It was totally sappy, totally illogical, and contrary to all she knew about stallions, but she hoped the Phantom would come say good-bye to his son.

Later, Sam glanced at her watch.

Thirty minutes had passed and the road was still empty.

Had Dr. Scott had trouble loading the colt? Even

tranquilized, Pirate wasn't likely to welcome the trailer's confinement. Sam swallowed, imagining his fear with walls on each side. The truck's engine would sound like a roaring beast he couldn't see out the front window, and he'd have no room to turn and see what was behind.

Suddenly, Sam saw Mrs. Allen's truck. From this distance, she imagined it was a meteor the size of a bowling ball, speeding this way to roll right over her. This could be a strange week.

Mrs. Allen was often cranky and picky, even about things that didn't matter. And Gabe mattered to her more than anything.

The one time Sam had talked with Gabe, he'd sounded smart and sure of himself, but bitter. He loved soccer and the accident had robbed him of another winning season.

Was it selfish to hope they'd both just leave her alone with Pirate? Yeah, it was.

Sam's hands tightened into fists as the orange truck drew nearer. It approached slowly, barely disturbing the dust cloud rising from the lane's powdery dirt.

"Shoot, Grandma, you didn't have to go so slow. You give new meaning to the words 'driving me crazy.'"

The male voice that drifted to Sam in the tree house was half gruff jock and half little kid.

They hadn't left the truck yet, so the windows

must be rolled down. Which meant she was sort of eavesdropping.

"Hi!" Sam shouted as she climbed down the tree house ladder, but neither of them seemed to hear.

"I got lots of your favorite foods," Mrs. Allen was saying. "Fried chicken, TV dinners, and green beans to make with onion rings on top."

"It's so hot, Grandma, sandwiches are fine with me," the voice said.

Even though Mrs. Allen was no cook, it sounded as if she wanted to do her best for her grandson. Added to what Gram had sent, they'd be eating well all week long, Sam thought.

"Hi!" Sam called again.

This time Mrs. Allen must have heard her, because she'd climbed down from the truck. She looked as she always did when dressed for town. Her dyed black hair was pulled back in a low ponytail, showing big silver concho earrings. Her white blouse was tucked into a long skirt.

One hand shaded her eyes as she looked toward Sam.

From this distance, Sam couldn't see the expression in Mrs. Allen's brown eyes, but she had a feeling the old woman's hand wasn't trembling from age.

*Hush . . . hush . . . hush.* Like the river's voice from her dream, the La Charla seemed to echo Dad's words.

*Don't go lookin' for trouble,* he'd said.

Sam drew a deep breath.

"Hi, Mrs. Allen!" she called.

Then, trying to be helpful, Sam darted forward to open the passenger's side door.

The guy inside had to be Gabe.

He looked like an athlete, with broad shoulders under a white team tee-shirt. His blond hair was short and prickly as porcupine quills. He wore a silver stud earring in one earlobe and had a grin so wide, his eyes were almost squinted closed.

He wore baggy black shorts, but his legs . . .

He'd been joking around until he saw her. Then the humor left Gabe's face in three quick shifts of expression. First his chin lifted, then his shoulders squared, making him look cocky and stuck-up. Next, his glance dropped to his legs and stayed there as if he couldn't look away from one leg in a cast from toes to mid-thigh and the other leg bruised with yellow bars and slashes.

When he managed to jerk his head up, Gabe looked vulnerable, completely defenseless as he waited for her reaction. Then his eyes turned green as a toxic chemical. As if his brain had barked an order to snap out of it, Gabe's sullen expression demanded, *Who the heck cares what you think?*

Sam had forgotten she was holding the door open for him until he gave it a flat-palmed thrust that vibrated through the metal into her fingers and wrist bone.

"Like I couldn't have opened it myself," he sneered.

Frozen by his fury, Sam pulled her hand away from the car door.

He reached into the backseat for crutches. He grunted, but there was no flailing around as he got them angled perfectly to lift himself upright.

"Sorry," she said, but she was remembering Dad's words all over again. She hadn't had to go looking for trouble. It had come looking for her.

## Chapter Seven

Gabe's hostile expression crinkled the scab over his cheekbone. He used the crutches to move closer. Way too close, in fact.

Sam stepped back. Afraid the tip of his crutch would crush her toe, she looked down. She'd tried not to, because she was certain Gabe would be self-conscious. But she did and noticed that though Gabe's bare leg looked muscular beneath the bruises, it dragged. The other leg swung a little bit, but only from the weight of its cast.

With a sick feeling, she realized Gabe hadn't regained the use of his legs. At least, not yet.

Sam wet her lips. How many words had passed between them during their single phone call? One hundred? Two? She didn't know him at all, but his stare dared her to say something.

"Gabriel," Mrs. Allen began, and her voice was shaky. "This is Samantha Forster from River Bend Ranch. I pointed out their bridge to you from the highway, remember? And you talked with her on the phone?"

"How are ya?" he asked. Sam felt a surge of hope. Maybe things would be okay, after all. But then Gabe's eyes flicked over her scornfully and he added, "I guess you're the official 'check out the gimp' greeting committee."

Did her mouth actually fall open?

In the single minute he'd been here, the guy had shoved a door at her, gotten—literally—in her face, and insulted her. Enough was enough.

"No," Sam snapped. "Actually, I've seen gimps before. But I'm waiting for a horse that's one of a kind."

Mrs. Allen gasped, but Gabe gave sort of a snort. His hands loosened their white-knuckled grip on his crutches. Even if it was rude, it might have been the right thing to say.

"Yeah?" Gabe stared toward the pasture and then the corral. "Looks to me like they can take care of themselves."

"Sam's going to be here all week," Mrs. Allen said. "He was a fine young horse—" Mrs. Allen broke off. Her hands fluttered in uncharacteristic dithering movements. "He was badly injured and it . . . she's . . ."

Mrs. Allen was holding back tears. Gabe's eyes narrowed with suspicion.

*Where'd Jen when I need her?* Sam wondered. Her best friend understood human psychology almost as well as she did that of horses. Maybe she'd compre-hend this guy's meanness.

"He's a mustang colt that was badly burned in that fire I told you about," Sam explained. She could hear the return of her own confidence. If there was one thing she could talk about, it was horses. "You know your grandmother takes in 'unadoptable' mus-tangs, and this one's not only been burned, he was traumatized, and is almost kind of crazy."

"Oh yeah, right," Gabe said.

Sam's eyes had wandered to the road, looking for Dr. Scott and Pirate, but Gabe's sarcasm drew her attention back.

"You don't believe me?" Sam asked, amazed.

"Why else would I be here?"

"To keep me company because you've done hos-pital time, too?" Gabe's sun-bleached eyebrows quirked up. He looked smug, as if she couldn't possi-bly deny his theory. "I don't suppose that could have anything to do with it?"

"I don't know how to break it to you, but—" Sam stopped. She'd been about to tell him he wasn't the center of her universe.

That would have crossed the line between sarcasm

and outright rudeness. Sam knew it, and Mrs. Allen's loud intake of breath underlined it.

The kid was being a jerk, but he had a good reason. Sam remembered when Rachel Slocum had spread a rumor about her all over school. Samantha Forster had suffered permanent brain damage from her riding accident, Rachel had told anyone who'd listen.

Despite the heat, the memory turned Sam's hands cold and she shivered with goose bumps. The stares—half of which she'd probably imagined—had tormented her. Hot blushes had lasted for days, like sunburn. She'd reacted—well, like she wasn't exactly sane.

At least that rumor had been false.

How must Gabe feel, knowing people were staring at him and seeing limp legs that had once been strong enough to kick a ball the entire length of a soccer field?

"That *could* have something to do with why I'm here, but it doesn't," Sam told him. "I'm here for the colt, because your grandma was willing to take him in and Dr. Scott—"

"The vet," Mrs. Allen put in.

"—talked me into working with the colt so he'd have a better chance of being adopted."

In the lull between sentences, Sam heard a faint nicker. Most of the wild horses had stopped grazing to stare toward the road, but she saw nothing.

"You could help her with the horse, though," Mrs. Allen said. Sam heard the apology in her words. Mrs. Allen had wanted to teach Gabe to ride this summer, but this might be the best she could offer.

"You could," Sam said slowly. An addition to Pirate's human herd might be a good idea.

"Oh yeah," Gabe snapped. "I'm totally set up to help you tame a wild horse." He shifted his weight to his left crutch and gestured with the right one. "Didn't anyone ever tell you it's not nice to tease the handicapped?"

Gabe was really feeling sorry for himself. Sam recognized the same bitterness she'd seen in Jake when he broke his leg. She understood, but she didn't have to like it.

She'd already opened her mouth to ask Mrs. Allen for help, when she heard the vet's truck.

"Here they come," Sam said. For a second, she wondered why her neck felt wobbly. Could it be from relief? Had she really been that tensed up?

Yes! Given the choice between facing a terrified, half-ton horse and a mixed-up guy, Sam knew she'd pick the horse, every time.

She could get inside the mind of a *loco* colt more easily than she could a guy who struck out at others just to prove he wasn't weak.

Mrs. Allen glanced at her watch. "Gabe, would you like to go inside? Maybe lie down on the couch for a little while?"

Gabe gave a curt shake of his head. "I want to check out this wild horse."

It took Sam only a second to see that Dr. Scott was following through on their plan to put Pirate in with the three saddle horses.

She gave Mrs. Allen a quick explanation, then bolted to open the pasture gate.

Dr. Scott backed up to the gate and turned the truck off.

"I should have bandaged his legs," Dr. Scott said before he uttered another word. "Or given him a higher dose of sedative."

The vet's eyes were pained, as if the banging around the colt had done in the trailer had bruised his flesh, too.

But Pirate was out of the trailer and into the corral in minutes.

"He knows what a pen's about," Mrs. Allen said, coming to stand beside the young vet.

"He should," Dr. Scott said, then squeezed Mrs. Allen's forearm. "Thanks so much, Trudy."

"For nothing," she said, shrugging.

Shimmering red gold in the morning sun, the colt pranced halfway around the corral, swerved away from the three saddle horses, then doubled back the way he'd come. Although Dr. Scott had said the colt hadn't lost vision in the eye with the starfish-shaped patch, Sam noticed that Pirate tilted his head, trying to keep his unmarred side to the other horses.

Now, as Calico advanced toward the colt, Sam recalled the mare's strength. Calico might be old, but Sam had spent an uncomfortable half hour once dangling from the pinto's halter rope as a farrier tried to shoe her.

But Calico only jostled against the colt's shoulder. The other paint mare, Ginger, clopped up to sniff him loudly, and no matter how the colt shied and tried to sidestep out of reach, she snuffled and rubbed him with her nose.

To establish his dominance, Judge slung his head over Pirate's neck. He didn't press downward, though, at least not enough that Sam could see it.

"They're all talking the same language," Dr. Scott said, and Sam could tell he was heartened by the horses' acceptance of the colt.

They were sweet and welcoming, just as they'd been with Ace when he'd spent his first minutes with them. Sam couldn't understand it. Turned into River Bend's saddle horse pasture, poor Pirate would have been reminded of his newcomer status with bites and kicks, not placid pressure and gentle nibbling.

Behind her, Sam heard Mrs. Allen talking quietly to Gabe.

"You're sure you're up to this? You've been awake for hours. You're not even in the same time zone."

"One hour difference is all," Gabe said, and when Sam glanced his way, he met her eyes.

She gave him a small smile for hanging in there, but Sam noticed his lips were pressed together hard and she thought a faint tremor showed in his arms as he arranged himself against the corral fence.

"I'll tell you a few things while he settles in," Dr. Scott said, coming to stand beside Sam. "We'll do show-and-tell afterward."

"Okay," Sam said, though she was thinking it would be polite if someone introduced Dr. Scott to Gabe.

It would be up to her, Sam thought, because Mrs. Allen was fussing over Gabe as if he were a little kid. And it was backfiring big time.

"Punishing fear is the biggest mistake you can make," Dr. Scott began, and Sam decided to let Gabe and the vet remain strangers for a while.

Dr. Scott was more interested in telling her how to handle the colt, and Gabe was trying to act tough, no matter what it cost him physically.

"Like we were talking about yesterday," Dr. Scott went on, "if you're not an equine mind reader, it's difficult to know exactly what triggers the memory of an old fear, but seeing it is easy."

"He's not scared now," Mrs. Allen said with self-assurance.

"No," Dr. Scott said, "and he's an easy one to read. He'll start twitching his tail as he becomes fearful. The more scared he gets, the faster that tail switches, until it's a blur."

"A blur," Sam echoed.

Dr. Scott nodded. "It's common to horses and cattle, but in him—"

The colt's front hooves did a stutter step.

"Yeah, I'm talkin' about you," the vet said in a voice that verged on baby talk, then made a smooching noise and the colt moved off. "Anyway, in him, it's like a fuse burning down."

Gabe gave a faint chuckle and Sam would bet he was imagining something like a round, black bomb in a cartoon, with a sparking fuse growing shorter and shorter as it burned. If Dr. Scott heard him, though, he gave no sign.

"Once he starts twitching his tail, it means he's having those memories again. One swish and you can keep doing what you're doing. Two swishes, get on your mark. Three, get set. Four, just get away fast."

Sam concentrated. That was easy enough, but she wondered what she was supposed to be doing while she was near him.

"Try to end the lesson before he's too scared," Dr. Scott emphasized.

"What lesson?" Sam asked.

The vet sighed. "That people are kind, that they won't hurt him. In fact, it'd be good if he started to believe people will even help him if they can. Then we've gotta hope the family he goes to reinforces the lesson."

The vet cleared his throat and continued in a

no-nonsense tone. "You want to work him no more than fifteen minutes at a time, but try to get in two hours per day."

Sam nodded. That didn't sound very hard. In fact, if Mrs. Allen didn't make her do any other chores, it would almost be a vacation.

In the corral, the horses had all come to a stop. Although the three saddle horses stood side by side facing the colt and he was a few steps away from them, all four animals' heads drooped in relaxation.

"So maybe I shouldn't do anything that makes his tail swish," Sam suggested.

"Well, we have to press him just a little bit if he's going to learn anything." Dr. Scott's words came out reluctantly. He pushed his black-rimmed glasses firmly up his nose. "It's kinda like this: Working with that colt is like watching a teakettle, and we want to keep him at a simmer. You know what that is?"

Sam did, but it was kind of hard to explain. "It's like, hot, but—sort of just before a boil?"

"Exactly!"

Dr. Scott jabbed an index finger her way. Again the colt startled. He sure was focused on the vet, Sam thought.

Behind her, Sam heard Gabe make an exclamation. She didn't hear exactly what he said, but she guessed he'd just now seen the colt's burned face.

"So, I should end his lessons before he reaches a full boil?" Sam asked the vet.

Dr. Scott hesitated for a second, then said, "Absolutely."

Sam nodded. She understood.

After the Phantom's capture and abuse by Karla Starr, Sam had mended her friendship with the stallion slowly and carefully.

Jaw jutting, Dr. Scott touched Sam's arm and guided her a few steps away from Mrs. Allen and Gabe.

"What?" she asked.

The young vet looked angrier than she'd ever seen him.

"How old's that kid?" Dr. Scott demanded.

"Gabriel? He's . . . I'm not sure. I think he's going to be a junior in high school. Why?"

"Since he's Trudy's grandson, I'll give him the benefit of the doubt, but he strikes me as a bad apple."

Sam had heard the expression before, but it didn't seem to fit. Gram said a bad apple was someone who, like a rotten apple in a barrel of tasty ones, spreads its decay. It didn't seem fair to dismiss Gabe as that sort of person.

"Why do you say that?" Sam asked.

"Once he saw the colt's burns, he couldn't stand to look at him. They're" —the vet shrugged— "unsightly, but he's still healing."

Dr. Scott gazed at the colt with affection.

"Gabe's kind of banged up himself," Sam said.

shrugging. "It seems like he'd understand what the colt's going through better than—"

"Stop it, Sam," Dr. Scott said grimly. "You know animals are sensitive to feelings. The colt's in a delicate stage of recovery. I think it'd be better for everyone if you kept that kid away from him."

The vet left her standing there and returned to his truck.

## Chapter Eight

r. Scott unloaded a big cardboard box full of supplies for the colt's care.

"We'll unpack it over here near the corral so he starts getting used to a little more activity than there was at my house," the vet said.

And lots more than there was on the range, Sam thought.

"First, you got your fifty packages of kiwi-strawberry Kool-Aid."

"What?" Sam said.

Dr. Scott was smiling. She hadn't heard him joke since the day they'd found the burned colt.

"It serves a couple of purposes," Dr. Scott explained as he rigged a battered blue plastic bucket to the side of the corral. He turned on the nearby hose. As he filled the bucket with water, he added two packages of the powder. "He likes the taste of it, so he drinks more and it keeps him hydrated. And since he'll be moving around—from my place, to here, to his new home—he won't develop a liking for the water at one particular place. It'll all taste the same to him."

"Good idea," Sam said. She remembered noticing how fresh and pure River Bend's well water tasted when she'd moved back from San Francisco. To horses, the difference would probably be even more obvious.

"We do it a lot with competition horses," Dr. Scott said, watching as the colt came toward the familiar bucket. "When you're moving from state to state, you can't take a chance of them getting dehydrated. There you go, boy," he crooned to the colt.

Pirate drank without looking down into the bucket. He stared over the rim, watching the humans.

"I keep a salt lick in there, too," Mrs. Allen pointed out. "That will help him stay thirsty."

The vet nodded, then pulled a tube of zinc oxide from the box.

"At this stage, sunburn can be serious. The skin around his eye and on his nose is regenerating."

As Dr. Scott made his way into the corral, he shot a quick look back over his shoulder at Gabe. Sam looked, too.

At first, as Dr. Scott pushed away the older horses and convinced the colt to let him approach, Gabe just looked interested. Then, after the vet had pulled on plastic gloves and began smoothing salve around the colt's nose and eye, Gabe's expression changed.

He squinted against the sun's glare, so she couldn't read his eyes, but Gabe didn't look grossed out. His lips pressed together and turned down at the corners. Beneath the slight vee of his hairline, his forehead creased in a frown.

He didn't seem to be pitying the colt, but . . . Sam tried not to stare. She faced away from Gabe, but kept her eyes rolled over as far as she could to watch him. Could he be holding his breath, staying as still as the colt was as Dr. Scott worked on him? If she had to guess, Sam would say Gabe was imagining the colt's pain.

"While it's hot like this, it would be best if he could get into the shade. Those trees will do," Dr. Scott said, nodding at the three cottonwoods on the side of the corral. "But watch the other horses. If they don't share, we'll have to move him."

"I plan to stay with him around the clock," Sam said. "I'm sleeping out here, too."

"Oh, now, Samantha," Mrs. Allen began. "It's not like it was with Faith."

"I brought my sleeping bag," Sam said.

"All right, then," Mrs. Allen agreed. "I know better

than to argue with one of you mule-stubborn Forsters."

Sam curbed her impulse to stick out her tongue. How totally immature would that have been? Besides, Mrs. Allen's weak joke had made everyone smile.

"That's it," Dr. Scott said, pulling off the plastic gloves and shoving them in a pocket. "We're pretty much past the stage where we have to worry overmuch about infection, but precautions won't hurt."

The colt's lips moved in a silent nicker as the vet closed the gate behind him. Dr. Scott didn't see it, but Sam did, and her heart ached for the young mustang.

"I brought plastic gloves for you to wear when you touch his face, and some flytraps to hang around here, and some fly spray," Dr. Scott said. He bent over the box, holding up each item as he mentioned it.

"You thought of a fly mask, I suppose," Mrs. Allen said.

Sam pictured the mesh hoods that slipped over a horse's head and ears to protect it from flies.

"I did, but he won't tolerate it," the vet said. "He refused to quit trying to paw it off. I could have hobbled him, but that would've caused a whole new set of problems."

Sam sucked in a breath. "That would be so scary for him. And he's already confined," she mused, "when he's used to running miles every day."

Gabe muttered something that was definitely sarcastic, and sounded like, "Imagine how that'd feel."

Sam set her teeth against one another to keep from talking. She knew Gabe was longing for his own hours of running, but couldn't he focus on the colt's problems, just for a little while?

"Now, I don't know what you've heard about the colt's, uh, episodes." Dr. Scott crossed his arms and looked thoughtful as he turned to Mrs. Allen.

"Brynna told me he goes a little crazy," Mrs. Allen said, "as if he's having bad memories."

"That's so," Dr. Scott agreed, "and you'll recognize it if it happens. If it does, it won't last long. Get out of his way, and when it ends, just treat him like a horse that's overheated. Sponge him off if you can. Squirt him with a hose if you have to, if he won't let you get close enough with the sponge. Quickest way to cool him down is to look for the big veins in his neck," Dr. Scott said, moving his hands down both sides of his own neck, "and inside his legs."

He waited a second until Sam nodded that she understood.

"Then scrape off the excess water so he won't get chilled while you walk him around."

When the vet looked down at her hands, Sam realized she'd laced her fingers together and was squeezing back and forth like a teeter-totter. She pulled her fingers away from one another and shook them out.

"I'll remember," she said quickly.

"I've written this all down for you, Sam," the vet

said, "just like I did before your buckskin foaled."

Thinking of the night Tempest was born made Sam sigh. She'd been all alone during that terrible storm, for the hours Sunny was foaling. She'd managed fine, and she could do this, too. The colt was counting on her.

"How long?" Gabe asked.

Everyone turned toward him in surprise, but no one said a word.

Gabe sounded impatient as he repeated, "How long does he need to be walked after he has an episode?"

"Until he feels cool to the touch between his front legs," the vet said.

He flashed Sam a look that said just maybe he'd been wrong about Gabe. For some reason, she felt herself smile.

"You're like a parent dropping off your child for his first day with a babysitter," Mrs. Allen told Dr. Scott.

"No," he said adamantly, "I'd just hate to see a patient fail."

"It's nothing to be ashamed of," Mrs. Allen said, brushing aside his protest. "But you needn't worry. I've seen this young lady at work with horses, and I know she'll do her best."

Pleased and embarrassed at the same time, Sam was about to thank Mrs. Allen for her vote of confidence, when Dr. Scott spoke up.

"I know that, and I've told her as much, but I

don't want her getting sidetracked." Dr. Scott aimed an accusing glance at Gabe.

The boy had the audacity to grin. Then he gave a shrug as if no female could help being distracted by him.

*Give me a break,* Sam thought. As everyone else looked amused, she flashed back to what Dr. Scott had said about a simmering teakettle. That was just how she felt, but she kept quiet.

"Well, of course, Gabe could help," Mrs. Allen offered. "He likes animals and he was hoping to learn to ride this summer."

"This'd be a good first step," Sam said, in spite of her irritation.

Dr. Scott lifted his shoulders stiffly, and though Sam was pretty sure he was thinking of Gabe's reaction to the colt's burns, Mrs. Allen totally misinterpreted the vet's gesture.

"Now, listen here," Mrs. Allen said, shaking her index finger at the young vet. "It's just a waiting game, this time with the crutches. He'll be better soon and in the meantime, he has enough strength in his upper body—from soccer, you know, throwing the ball in from the sidelines. Isn't that right, Gabe?" She didn't give him a chance to agree, but Sam glanced over at him. He looked pained and angry, but reluctant to tell his grandmother to hush. "Those muscles in his shoulders are why he's able to get around on crutches, when most people in his situation would be confined to a wheelchair."

Thank goodness Mrs. Allen ran out of breath, because Gabe looked pale, and perspiration glimmered on his face.

"A soccer player, are you?" Dr. Scott asked. Gabe gave a stiff nod. "You might like this, then." The vet lifted a big rubber ball from the box. It had black-and-white pentagons on it like a soccer ball, but it was egg-shaped and had a handle on top. "It's a horse ball, and he loves it. He's stopped beating up his water bucket since I gave it to him. He tosses it all over his pen, and since it's not round, it bounces funny. Nothing like this out on the range, is there, boy?"

The colt's ears flicked to catch the vet's words. Hearing his own enthusiasm, Dr. Scott cleared his throat. "Now, Sam, I'll just take you inside the corral for an introduction and then I've got to be on my way."

"Why don't we go inside and get you settled," Mrs. Allen said to Gabe.

"What?" His tone was astonished, despite his shocky look. "Go inside?"

Sam knew she would have felt the same. It would be like missing a mini-rodeo. But missing what would probably be her humiliation by the wild horse wasn't the worst of it.

Hands on the hips of her black skirt, head tilted to one side as if she was about to say something fun and sassy, Mrs. Allen added, "Go on, Gabe, I'll even give you a head start."

## *Chapter Nine*

G'll *even give you a head start?* How could Mrs. Allen look at her sixteen-year-old grandson on crutches he despised and say that?

How could she forget that the wrought-iron gate was tricky, the garden path rough, and the heavy wooden front door—once you got it opened—was guarded by Imp and Angel?

Sam winced for both of them. Mrs. Allen had said the words lightly, like you'd tell a little kid you'd give him a head start in a footrace. Gabe's face turned red and Sam could only guess what he was thinking. Maybe that if his condition didn't improve, there'd be hundreds of moments like this? Cruelty cut deep, even if it was accidental.

Sympathy clouded Sam's excitement as she walked toward the gate, but she tried to shake it off. If Gabe was anything like Jake, he'd hate being pitied.

"Keep watching and you might see me get trampled," Sam called to him.

"You can't think that would be entertaining," Mrs. Allen said. She frowned with nervous concern, but Sam gave her a smile.

Though Gabe didn't say anything, Sam thought his expression looked a little less tight.

Sam had reached the gate when she noticed that Dr. Scott wasn't with her. He'd stopped at the loud staticky sound followed by garbled words that came from his truck. He stood with tilted head, listening.

"That's my CB radio," he explained, then nodded at a pattern of beeps. "Yep, and that's my tone."

Dr. Scott jogged over to his truck and began making notes on a clipboard before he strode back, clearly in a hurry.

"'Fraid I've got to go before I make the introductions," he said, nodding toward the colt in the corral. "Got a rancher who pulled a cow out of the mud yesterday and today she can't hold her head up. Something's wrong with her neck." Dr. Scott made an exasperated gesture. "You can't just haul an animal around by its head. The spinal cord is delicate, you know?"

"Yeah," Sam said weakly, but she was wondering if that was what was wrong with Gabe.

"Don't go inside the corral without a spotter—someone who can get help if you need it," Dr. Scott said. "That's a flat-out law, understand?"

Sam nodded. Pirate was pretty calm with Dr. Scott here, but what would happen when he left?

"I don't plan to try until tomorrow," she said. "I'll just hang around outside the corral and let him get used to me, today."

"Good plan," he said, then glanced at the box of supplies. "Well, I think you have everything you'll need. I'd best be going."

"I'll walk out with you," Mrs. Allen said. She sounded eager to escape her cranky grandson, and it seemed to Sam that Gabe relaxed a little, too, as his grandmother moved away.

"It's kind of hard to be nice, I bet," Sam sympathized.

Gabe started to nod, then shrugged as if it didn't matter.

Mrs. Allen's black skirts swished back from her dressy boots as she matched steps with the young vet. Her dark head was bent toward Dr. Scott's blond one as if she was glad for adult company.

Some people just aren't cut out to live with teenagers, Sam thought.

Dr. Scott's voice was a low rumble, but Sam was pretty sure he'd said something to Mrs. Allen about having her hands full.

"I'm going to keep him busy, and not let him

brood." Mrs. Allen's determined voice came to them clearly. Gabe readjusted his position on the crutches and made a frustrated sound as his grandmother went on, ". . . a waiting game and we're all on the verge of pulling our hair out, wondering—"

"You can talk about this in front of me, you know!" Gabe shouted, trying to sound overly patient. "I'd like that a lot better."

Mrs. Allen turned. For an instant, both hands covered her mouth.

"Oh, now I've hurt her feelings," Gabe moaned. "This isn't going to work."

"Are you hungry?" Sam asked suddenly.

"What?" First he looked surprised, then disgusted. "I can't believe—"

"Hey," Sam said, holding up her hands as if she'd halt him. "That's *my* grandmother's remedy for everything. I've had a warped childhood, so don't blame me. See all that stuff?" Sam pointed to the paper bag and Styrofoam cooler. "It's food. There are some cinnamon rolls she made this morning that we really should eat."

"Should," Gabe echoed.

"They're not like the ones you buy," Sam said.

She squatted, lifted the cooler's lid, and unfolded an edge of the aluminum enclosing the pastry. The smell of cinnamon reminded her that hours had passed since she'd spooned down her breakfast cereal.

"They smell good," Gabe admitted, and Sam was pretty sure she heard his stomach growl.

"They're still warm, now, but they'll be hard as rocks in a couple of hours," Sam told him, then glanced over at the scuff of boots.

"What's this, now? Grace doesn't think I'm capable of providing food for my own grandson?" Mrs. Allen demanded as she walked back toward them, but she didn't sound genuinely insulted.

"Gram can't help herself," Sam said, and when Mrs. Allen chuckled, it was clear she was still happy she'd rekindled her old friendship with Gram, and clearer still that she welcomed even a minute's break from worrying about Gabe, so Sam teased her a bit. "You're lucky she didn't come over and start banging around pots and pans in your kitchen."

"Well," Mrs. Allen said. "That wouldn't be the curse of the century. I've never known that woman to cook anything that wasn't delicious. Maybe we'd better go inside and eat those cinnamon rolls before they set up."

Mrs. Allen hurried ahead of them to move the Boston bulldogs from the house into her art studio. "It'll just be easier," she'd said, and though Gabe had nodded in agreement, Sam had seen him lick his lips and look a little sad. She'd bet he liked those two nutty little dogs.

Sam walked beside him to the door, and before they reached the front step, Mrs. Allen was back, opening the heavy wooden door to them with a flourish.

"Welcome," she said, then stepped back as Gabe made his way inside.

"Your house is different," Gabe said as he crossed the entrance hall and lowered himself into a chair at the cluttered mahogany table.

How old had Gabe been the last time he'd entered this room? According to Gram, Mrs. Allen had neglected her friends and family, placing her art above them for years. But after her husband's death, she'd rebuilt those relationships.

"I haven't changed a thing," Mrs. Allen said, and the tension returned to her face. "Ever." Hands on her hips, she looked around, confused, but Sam knew what Gabe meant.

The first time she'd entered the house, heavy drapes had covered the tall windows. Now they were pushed back to show sunny views of sagebrush-covered range and the Calico Mountains. If Sam craned her neck just right, she could see green swathes of pasture dotted with captive mustangs.

That first day, the smell of medicine had permeated the rooms. Now, fragrance drifted from china bowls of rose petals, and the lingering salt and butter smell of popcorn had settled around the microwave oven.

There was another smell, too, Sam realized. Something like barbecue smoke.

"You used to have some scary paintings," Gabe said. "Of flowers with teeth."

"They're not scary, just accurate," Mrs. Allen said. She folded her arms, instantly defensive of her artwork, which depicted carnivorous plants. "And my agent said they're unique, and enjoying quite a little popularity with some collectors."

Gabe's eyes swung to meet Sam's. For one moment, Sam thought they'd both burst into laughter, but the feeling passed, and Sam helped Mrs. Allen get down saucers for the cinnamon rolls and glasses for milk.

Once they'd all exclaimed over the delicious rolls, they ate in silence.

Sam glanced toward the ivory-and-brass telephone on the round table draped with a gypsy-looking scarf. When she'd talked with Gabe that night when he was still in the hospital, they'd sort of understood each other. But not now.

"You probably want to know about my accident," Gabe said in an accusing tone.

"It's none of my business," Sam said. "Besides, your grandmother was telling you the truth. I'm just here to help with the colt."

"So you don't want to know. You think it would gross you out?"

Then, before Sam could protest, he changed the subject. "If you know so much about horses, how come you're calling that one a colt, when he's practically grown up?" Gabe stopped for a breath and added, "Isn't a colt a baby?"

Sam looked to Mrs. Allen, expecting her to take over, but maybe things were piling up on her, and Mrs. Allen was taking a break, because she appeared engrossed in unrolling her pastry to get to its tender center.

"I *do* want to know," Sam said. "It was really awful when I was down painting your grandmother's fence and she drove up to tell me you'd been in an accident and I could tell from her voice she didn't even know if you'd live."

Gabe turned to his grandmother and took a shuddering breath. Mrs. Allen didn't look up from her fork, which was skimming white frosting from her roll.

"And a colt is a male horse under four years old," Sam told him.

"Lecture me," Gabe taunted. "I really like that from a younger kid."

Sam ignored him and added, "That mustang is probably only a yearling. So he qualifies. And don't you want to know his story?"

"I know it," Gabe said, and his voice sounded nice, finally. "You told me, that night."

*Progress*, Sam thought, as Gabe glanced toward his grandmother's phone. *He at least admits we've talked before.*

"So, you were on a road trip?" Sam coaxed him to

talk about it, not sure why she wanted to know.

"Yeah, three of us. We had this plan. We all play soccer and we're all, like, C+ students, so we've been getting our grades up. Then all of us were going to just shine during our junior and senior seasons, and apply for college scholarships at the same school." Gabe paused and rubbed his battered right knee. "We all have June birthdays, too, and we got our licenses just—bing, bing, bing. Three in a row. We were surprised when our parents said we could take off on our own for the weekend, but those good end-of-the-year grades did it. The trip was like a reward."

"But there were rules," Mrs. Allen pointed out.

They both looked at her, but she still watched her fork. Now she pressed it down on crumbs, like she was seeing how many she could pick up.

"Yeah, like we were supposed to stay in a motel overnight," Gabe said. "My dad made the reservation. But we weren't tired, and so we took turns driving, thinking we could get to Salt Lake City by morning."

"What were you going to do there?" Sam asked.

"Nothing," Gabe said, shaking his head. "Go see a girl my friend Yogi met during spring break last year."

"Yogi?" Sam asked, with a laugh.

Then she stopped. What if Yogi hadn't survived the accident? Her mind raced, trying to remember if she knew what had happened to the other boys.

"He's okay except for a broken finger," Gabe told her. "So is Luis, my other friend. He dislocated his shoulder, but they mainly got cuts and bruises. That's what would've happened to me if I'd been driving or sitting in the backseat, but I had to call shotgun."

Sam pictured the teenage boys piling into the car and Gabe taking the front passenger's seat.

"And even that would've been okay if I'd stayed awake and reached for the CD that Yogi wanted, but I fell asleep and he . . ."

Sam imagined the boy trying to drive and reach for something, too. She didn't drive yet, but she could imagine veering off the road if you tried to do both at the same time.

"It sounds like it was his fault," Sam said.

"You don't even know him," Gabe snapped.

"You're right." Sam hurried to say it. She knew better than to criticize people's friends. If Jen had done something wrong, Sam knew she'd stand up for her to other people.

"But then . . ." Gabe's eyes took on a faraway expression before he recited the next part and Mrs. Allen finally looked up, as if she couldn't not pay attention, although she had to know what had happened. "Yogi veered over into the other lane, and overcorrected, and the car rolled. My seat got the worst of it. The front of the car crushed against my legs, but that was kind of good, because they were bleeding and the metal actually sort of acted like a tourniquet, so I didn't bleed to death, but it also did something to my spine. And like your horse doctor said, you really don't want to be messing with the spine."

Gabe's hands covered his face, then moved as if he were washing it. Maybe he was, Sam thought, washing away memories of being trapped.

"So, they cut open the car with the 'jaws of life'— like a chain saw that'll cut through cars—and told me how lucky I was to be alive. They took me to the hospital and I don't remember a couple days, except when I woke up, everyone started in with the 'lucky' stuff again. I'm lucky to have the upper body strength to go on crutches instead of be in a wheelchair, lucky they could fix this leg with a steel rod," he said, knocking on the plaster cast, "and lucky that I might not lose the use of this other leg, the beat-up one, because there's still some mobility—"

He broke off, and when he resumed talking, he sounded almost robotic. "It's a waiting game, like my grandmother said. We just wait until the swelling goes down and if I'm lucky again, I'll be able to use both legs like before. If it turns out I've used up all my freakin' good luck—" Gabe held his hands palm up, one to each side. "What ya see is what I've got."

"He's perfectly stable, otherwise." Mrs. Allen tried to sound cheery, but her hands were pressed palm down on the table, flanking the plate with the unrolled but uneaten cinnamon roll." "And the doctor's encouraged him to be up and around and active."

"Don't think I don't know why," Gabe said. "The doctor was cool. She told me everything."

Mrs. Allen gave a nod of agreement. "The doctor said she wished she could tell him everything would be okay, and she really seems to believe it will," Mrs. Allen said adamantly. "But she can't promise. And she did mention that with a chronic condition like this, even the sweetest people in the world can't help but be angry."

"And I wasn't sweet to begin with," Gabe said. He sat back with his arms crossed, trying to look tough, but Sam could see his hands shaking.

"Of course you were. When you were training for soccer and going to school and falling into bed exhausted, you were perfectly sweet." Mrs. Allen's chin lifted and her eyes narrowed. She looked as if she'd had enough.

She stood up, cleared the dishes to the kitchen sink, and continued, "Now, I'm going to get things settled in your room. Whether you realize it or not, you need a rest."

"Look," Gabe said, turning his anger on his grandmother.

Mrs. Allen was ready for it.

"*You* look," Mrs. Allen snapped, with the nerve Sam had always admired. "I know very well you agreed to come visit not because you wanted to be with me, or be around horses, like you said, but because you wanted to get away from your friends. *They're* getting ready for school and soccer, and—at least in your mind—pitying you because you'll miss this season, entirely."

"Grandma!" Gabe's mouth stayed open as if he couldn't go on.

"There's no point in us lying to each other," Mrs. Allen said. She held Gabe's gym bag in one hand and a backpack bulging with square shapes that must be books in the other. Even though the strap of a pair of binoculars was wrapped around her wrist, too, she looked balanced and in control.

"It's the truth. Now that you're here, though, you're going to get better. I'm going to make you get better!" Mrs. Allen leaned toward him, voice lowered. "Your upper body works just fine and so does your brain. You're a young athlete who's had some bad luck, just like that horse. You know what he's going through, and you'll help Samantha bring him back to what he should be."

Sam sat very still. Mrs. Allen's quiet voice was scarier than her shouting. Sam didn't want to attract Mrs. Allen's attention, but Sam couldn't let her hope for something that was practically a miracle.

"Mrs. Allen?" Sam began cautiously.

Mrs. Allen's silver concho earrings flashed like lightning. She whirled so quickly, a lock of black hair came loose and fell over one eye.

"You can hush, too, Samantha. I took that colt in when I already had way too much on my plate. You knew it, so did your whole family and young Dr. Scott. Well, this is how I'm going to make everything work. This is the price you'll pay to save him!"

"Wait—"

"But—"

Mrs. Allen refused to listen to either of them.

"Both of you sit quietly and see if you can wrap your minds around this: For the next five days you'll work together on that colt or all three of you are out of here."

As if she'd been pounding on a piano and suddenly stopped, vibration hung in the room. Mrs. Allen cleared her throat and flashed a smile too bright and giddy for a seventy-something lady.

"Now." Mrs. Allen's voice was barely audible. "If there are no questions, I think I'll go make up the bed in the guest room."

Sam took a deep breath and stared after her, listening until she no longer heard the swishing skirts and thumping boot heels.

If Brynna and Dr. Scott thought Pirate was crazy, they should come spend some time with Mrs. Allen. Next to her, the *loco* little horse seemed absolutely serene.

## Chapter Ten

"I'm going to go outside and sit with the colt," Sam told Gabe once Mrs. Allen was busy in the other room.

"Sure, leave me in here with her."

"She's your grandmother," Sam said, smiling.

"Mine just cooks too much."

"You think this is funny?" Gabe asked, rubbing one hand over his spiky hair.

"A little bit," she admitted. Now that Mrs. Allen was out of the room, it all made sense. Sam had seen the tension building in the older woman since she climbed down from her tangerine-colored truck. "I think she's just worried about you, and this is how she's showing it."

"By acting crazy? What about creating a secure environment for the invalid?" Gabe asked, then lowered his voice. "I haven't been around her that much. We were just getting to know each other before this happened. I—"

Gabe broke off. Then, looking thoughtful, he reached up and turned the gold stud in his earlobe. "If I'd come out here to visit when she wanted me to, two weeks ago, I wouldn't have been on that road trip."

Sam remembered the long list of "ifs" from her own accident. If she'd paid closer attention to her horse, to the weather, to Jake's technique of riding through the gate, to any of those things, she might not have fallen and the horse she loved wouldn't have escaped.

But it didn't matter how many "ifs" she listed. She'd made a mistake that had caused her to fall. The stallion's hoof had grazed her head. He'd run for the mountains, leaving her on the ground, where she heard his hooves retreating into silence.

Even if she could count off ten thousand ways she might have changed that day, it was too late. But she sure wasn't going to lecture Gabe about the lessons she'd learned. Sooner or later, he'd learn them for himself.

"So, do you want to learn to ride?" Sam asked.

Gabe's expression said she didn't deserve an answer, so Sam didn't wait for one.

"The first step to horsemanship is always done on the ground anyway. You need to get to know the horse. They're individuals just like people, in how they think, how they understand the world, and how they express themselves."

Gabe still didn't say anything. Given the way he sagged against his forearms, which lay on the mahogany table, Sam guessed his silence wasn't all resentment. Part of it was weariness. Just the same, he was listening.

Sam told him about the HARP program, going over the days of groundwork that preceded actually mounting the mustangs. She talked about the program's success with girls like Mikki Small and the failures that had come before the successes.

"You let them burn down your barn, get bitten by snakes, and commit, like, Internet fraud. Then, instead of suing them," Gabe asked, "you talk about them being scared and getting over it? That's lame."

Shaking his head, Gabe leaned forward until his chin rested on his folded arms.

"Maybe," Sam said. "But it works."

Gabe's eyelids were drooping. Careful that her chair didn't squeak as she pushed back from the table, Sam slipped out of the kitchen, through the door, and onto the rose-flanked walk.

Bees zipped between flowers. Sunbeams high-lighted small bodies the color of orange marmalade and striped with black. No sultry breeze hinted of rain or rocked the roses on their thorned stems. It was still and silent except for the bees' droning.

Sam hoped the horses were dozing in the pen, feeling relaxed and accepting. She tried to open the iron gate soundlessly, but one glance across the ranch yard told her she needn't have bothered.

The colt was already watching her. The saddle horses were ranged against the far fence, in the shade of the cottonwood tree. Judge and Ginger stood head to tail, dozing. Calico's chin pointed up as she rubbed her neck against the fence, scratching an itch on the top board.

If Pirate backed a single step, his tail would brush one of the other horses. Even in the security of this small herd, though, his body was tense and his ears pricked to catch each of her footfalls.

"Hey, baby," Sam crooned when she was still halfway across the yard from the corral. "I bet you had me the minute I opened the door, didn't you?"

The colt's head bowed, then jerked up. He was probably dodging a fly, but his black mane swayed forward on his glossy neck and he looked like he was agreeing.

"You'd be long gone if not for those fences. Is that what you're thinking?" Sam asked him, but as she did, she reached one hand out.

Hooves stuttered, kicking up sand as the yearling threw himself sideways to escape. His bay hide slammed against the other horses, earning him flattened ears and bared teeth. Eyes rolling, he skittered off a few steps, then turned his tail to her, still trembling and completely aware of her movements.

*No!* She'd already committed two mistakes— reaching out and talking.

How had she forgotten that the mustang's world had nothing—at least nothing friendly—with arms. Cougars had long, clutching arms that ended in claws. Men had arms that ended in snaking ropes. Yes, Dr. Scott had reached out to pet and heal the colt, but Sam was new and strange. The colt had relied on his wild instincts to assess her.

Crooning to the colt as she approached so that he wasn't surprised by her sudden appearance would have been fine, except he'd already known she was coming. He'd been watching her, so she should have stayed silent.

Wild horses were prey. Safety meant communicating with widened eyes, flicking ears, and flared nostrils. Translated into human terms, she'd just bounded into someone's house bellowing an offer to mug them.

*And I have an unparalleled knack with horses,* Sam thought. Yeah, right.

Since she'd already disrupted naptime, Sam circled to the far side of the corral. All of the horses moved away until she sat on the ground, cross-legged in the shade. Then Mrs. Allen's three horses returned. Calico sniffed along the bottom rail. She turned her head sideways and fluttered her lips over Sam's hand.

"Good girl," Sam whispered. She used her knuckles to stroke the velvety skin between the mare's nostrils.

Calico enjoyed the caress for a few seconds, then snorted, hinting that a treat would be appropriate about now. But Sam had nothing to offer the pinto mare, so Calico huffed, moved off a few dragging steps, and closed her blond eyelashes for a nap.

Pirate stood as far from Sam as he could, with his shoulder, barrel, and hip pressed against the fence rail. But his neck wrinkled, showing amber-red glints, as his head turned to watch her.

If only he could read her mind, the colt would know he had nothing to fear. But, Sam thought, probably every kind human who'd ever worked with a frightened horse had made the same wish.

The best she could hope for was that Pirate believed the endorsement of the other horses. They stood nearby and though she knew their presence had more to do with the change than companionship, Calico *had* asked for her touch. The colt must have noticed.

Sweat gathered on Sam's forehead and dribbled down her temples and cheeks. She closed her eyes to keep the saltiness out, and wished she could flap her collar to cool her hot neck and throat. But the colt would probably think she was some weird, squatting bird of prey.

She'd been sitting in this cross-legged position so long that she was pretty sure the wrinkles in her jeans had made permanent indentations on her legs. The indigo dye had probably soaked into her skin cells, making her blue-legged forever.

Tiny wings whirred past her ear. Sam didn't flinch, but she felt exposed. Because she was hatless, that dragonfly could dive-bomb her head, or—what was it they were rumored to do?—sew up her ears.

*Crunch.*

Sam lifted her eyelashes, millimeter by millimeter.

Pirate had taken one step away from the corral fence, then another, then rushed to sling his head over Ginger's back for comfort. The old mare flattened her ears, but she didn't move away. She'd put up with the yearling, she seemed to say, if he'd just stay still.

Sam watched the colt and he watched her. She considered his white salved nose and eye area and wondered if the smooth pink skin underneath would ever grow hair again.

Hours later, when her patch of shade had moved with the traveling sun, Sam measured her progress by the colt's hipshot stance. His head drooped and one rear hoof was cocked on its tip. She didn't dare move, even when the iron gate creaked and she saw Mrs. Allen coming toward her.

The older woman had changed into a sleeveless blue dress and she wore something amazing on her head. It was sort of a cross between a vaquero's flat brimmed hat and something a Southern belle would wear. It was as big as an extra, extra-large pizza. Sam had never seen anything like it.

Neither had Pirate. The yearling threw his head up and began backing, nostrils wide. When he bumped Judge, the old bay swiveled one ear toward the sight, heard nothing threatening, then gave an impatient swish of his tail as if the colt had wakened him for nothing.

Just the same, Pirate crowded past the other horses, getting as far from Mrs. Allen as he could.

Not Sam. She'd just noticed Mrs. Allen was carrying a frosty glass. With luck, it was for her.

"Oh honey," Mrs. Allen said. She stopped beside Sam and looked down at her, tsking her tongue. "That colt's not the only one that needs sunscreen. You should have put some on yourself."

Why hadn't she thought of that? Sam wondered. Her face did feel kind of hot and tight.

"You are sunburned red as a clown's nose. Hope you're all finished peeling by the time school starts up again."

"Me too," Sam said, and it seemed her lips cracked just from talking.

A meadow lark caroled from one of the fields and Calico plunged her nose into the watering trough, then made a breathy, splashing sound like a surfacing whale.

"How's he doing?" Mrs. Allen asked, nodding at the colt.

Standing slowly, because her knees had locked and she had to work to straighten them, Sam drank the lemonade Mrs. Allen had brought her, while she explained what she'd observed.

After ten minutes of description, Sam summed it up. "He's skittish, but not terrified. I think after we spend a little time together, he'll be used to me."

"Same could be said for me and Gabe."

Sam looked away from the colt to make sure Mrs. Allen was joking.

"You *can* use him with the colt, can't you?" Mrs. Allen asked.

"Gabe? Sure," Sam said adamantly. "Just like we do with the HARP girls, before they ride. It's all groundwork. I told him about it."

"And?"

"He didn't have much to say," Sam told her.

"Well, I think the time for talking is done. Action's what's gonna make him well. If he can help heal that horse, he'll feel better, too."

"Sounds good to me," Sam said.

"That's how it is with men," Mrs. Allen went on, as if Sam hadn't spoken. "In fact, I'm thinking I might get that Jake Ely to come over if he has a minute between working for that father of his and that step-mother of yours."

Sam sighed. Jake and Gabe were both guys, and they'd both been injured, but she couldn't see the two bonding. She'd already told Mrs. Allen her opinion. Clearly, Gabe's grandmother thought she knew best.

"Now, I'm not so sure that sleeping bag's a good idea," Mrs. Allen said, nodding at Sam's bedroll. "Oh, it'll be cooler, and you'll be closer to the horses, and all," she agreed when Sam started to protest. "Only thing is the snakes."

"Snakes?" Sam's legs molded together, her arms crossed so that her palms touched the tops of her shoulders and she looked at the ground beneath her feet and for yards around.

"Country girl like you shouldn't be afraid of snakes," Mrs. Allen chided.

This time last year, Sam would have agreed, but years of idle warnings had finally turned into reality in June. Sam had nearly stepped on a rattlesnake sunning itself outside their new bunkhouse. She'd seen a garter snake grab onto a girl's hand and grind with its tiny serrated jaws, too.

She was in no rush to share her sleeping bag with any snake, venomous or not. So when Mrs. Allen offered her a hammock and helped her hang it between the two cottonwood trees next to the corral, she thought it was the best idea she'd heard in weeks and Sam was sure she'd sleep more soundly.

Gabe slept through dinner, and even though Sam romped Imp and Angel, who were crazy from being locked in Mrs. Allen's studio all day, then watched television for an hour with Mrs. Allen, Gabe still hadn't stirred.

"Think I should wake him up so he can eat some-thing?" Mrs. Allen asked when Sam headed for the door.

Sam shrugged and opened the door. A heavy scent of roses flowed inside from the garden as Sam said, "I have no clue."

"Probably tells you what kind of mother I was that I haven't a clue either," Mrs. Allen said.

"I bet you were lots of fun," Sam told her.

"No, I wasn't," Mrs. Allen's voice was flat. "But I've got a second chance to do things right and I won't waste it."

Just as Sam's arms had acted without her permission when she gestured to the colt, they reached around Mrs. Allen's thin shoulders and gave her a hug.

*Where did that come from?* Sam asked herself, but Mrs. Allen looked so pleased, Sam pretended she'd meant to do it.

"Well, now, isn't that nice," Mrs. Allen said, flustered. Then she looked around the kitchen and the living room. "One thing I do know about mothering is that the microwave pasta I gave you isn't exactly packed with nutrition."

"Oh, that's okay. I get plenty of nutrition at home."

Mrs. Allen laughed, and Sam grimaced. That hadn't come out the way she'd meant it to.

"I want you to take a few of these," Mrs. Allen

said, taking a colander full of peaches from inside the refrigerator. "Some fella was selling them outta the back of his truck in Alkali. They're good for you and they can count as dessert, too."

Sam took the first peach she touched, though it felt kind of soft. It might have been around for a little while, Sam thought, but she didn't care. It was cold enough that she could rub it on her sunburned cheeks, if nothing else.

"Now, my outside lights are on a timer," Mrs. Allen said, touching Sam's arm before she made it through the door. "And since I don't keep hens anymore and don't need those lights to keep away coyotes, they go off at midnight. Is that going to be okay with you?"

"Fine," Sam said. "I like to be able to see the stars."

"Nighty night, then," Mrs. Allen said.

At last, Sam was ready to sleep. All the commotion she'd made climbing into the hammock disturbed the horses, and Pirate was trotting circles around and around the corral.

Knowing her voice probably wouldn't soothe him, Sam just listened. She heard a cow with a hooting moo far off on the range, and the colt's frantic hooves. She heard the silken rustle of an owl swooping overhead, and circling hooves. She heard a lone coyote's howl, followed by a chorus of yaps. Even the wildlife couldn't sleep in this heat.

Then she realized the colt had stopped circling. She tried to believe Pirate had just grown weary. She told herself it was silly to imagine the Phantom was near. But some instinct crackled like electricity through Sam's veins. He *was* here. She just knew it.

The hammock rocked crazily as she sat up. With one hand on each side of the hammock, she balanced and listened. Nothing. She opened her eyes as wide as they could go, staring through the darkness toward the corral.

The moon didn't lend much light, but she saw the colt's dark outline and almost felt his trembling as he nickered toward the open range.

*Chapter Eleven* ♋

$C$oyotes were still out romping. That meant mustangs could be, too.

Grabbing each side of the hammock, Sam slung one leg over the edge, balanced, then dragged the leg out without falling.

Glad she'd gone to bed in shorts and a T-shirt but frustrated that she had to waste precious seconds putting on shoes, Sam grabbed the sneakers she'd stashed beneath the hammock. Mrs. Allen's warning had made Sam nervous, but it was her own gruesome fantasy of stepping on a fangs-bared rattlesnake that kept her from rushing into the night barefooted.

As Sam sat down and pulled on the sneakers, she had a moment to think.

Where was the stallion? What kind of terrain would she have to sprint across to get to him? She didn't know the anthills, rabbit brush, or dry, pebble-filled washes of Deerpath Ranch one tenth as well as she did the landscape of River Bend. She pulled the laces tight and double-knotted them.

Sam glanced over at the yearling.

The glowing half-moon showed everything in shades of gray. In silhouette, Pirate looked a lot like the Phantom. Loosed from the corral, Pirate could lead her to his home herd and she could ride behind him on Calico, or —

No. Sam couldn't believe that selfish thought had even crossed her mind. She wanted to apologize to the colt as he stood, head held high, amid a cage of shadows from fence posts and cottonwood branches. Because his lungs had been damaged by smoke inhalation, he wouldn't survive the high desert winters. Letting him lead her back for just an hour or two would have been cruel.

The colt sniffed loudly, searching the still night air for clues to what he'd heard.

Shoes tied, Sam stood with hands on hips and wished she could ask him for a hint.

The mustang pasture seemed the most likely place to find the Phantom, but was the presence of other horses enough to make the silver stallion forget the fire, exploding paint cans, and a week of captivity? Pirate was proof that horses could have bad memories, so maybe the Phantom wouldn't return there. Where else could she find him?

Sam remembered the week she'd stayed on Deerpath Ranch watching over Faith, the blind filly. One night the Phantom had hidden in the overgrown brush flanking the road and charged Jake. But the tall weeds had been cut back long ago.

Sam tapped her fingertips against the shorts covering her thighs. If she didn't hurry, he'd be gone.

The only other place she'd seen the stallion was the hot springs beyond the tree house. That had to be a mile away. She wasn't certain she could find it. She'd ended up there in a snowstorm because Calico had been attracted by the stallion as he stood guard over Faith.

Now, darkness cloaked the landmarks she might remember.

"Do something," Sam muttered to herself.

As she took a step, Sam caught a whiff of the peach from Mrs. Allen's kitchen.

Did horses like peaches? She'd find out. If its sweet scent carried to the Phantom, maybe she wouldn't have to know where to find him. Maybe he'd come to her.

Sam walked toward the mustang pasture, hoping they'd give her a sign. If the stallion had brought his entire herd, the captive horses would definitely be looking at them.

Dry grass crunched under Sam's shoes. She

hurried, jogging, walking, then jogging again. When she stopped to catch her breath, a crunch sounded nearby.

What was out here with her?

Nothing but her imagination indicated that the Phantom was nearby.

Maybe Pirate hadn't heard horses at all. He was a prey animal. He could have heard a cougar, a bobcat, or even a lone coyote that had strayed from the pack she'd heard howling.

Mrs. Allen's bluish yard lights were supposed to keep coyotes away, but they were off for the night. Sam strained, listening for canine pads moving over the dry grass.

Then Sam recalled the colt's longing nicker and she almost laughed with relief. He wouldn't signal a predator. He had to be calling to another horse.

What if the Phantom had come looking for Pirate? Sam drew a deep breath and released it in tiny increments. What if the silver-white stallion had been neighing across the fire-blackened range, looking for his son?

It made a pretty picture in her imagination, but Sam wouldn't breathe a word of the idea to anyone who knew horses. Jen and Jake would gape at her as if she'd lost her mind. Brynna the biologist would regret the hours she'd wasted explaining everything she knew about wild horses to her mush-minded stepdaughter.

*Don't be silly,* Sam lectured herself. No stallion would come searching for a young male. The Phantom would have driven the colt from the herd in a year or two, anyway, before he could make a challenge for supremacy.

Sam approached the mustang corral with determined steps. Only a few horses were in sight. Just before she reached the pasture fence, she heard a squawk. It must be breezier than she'd thought, because that sounded like the creaky hinge on Mrs. Allen's garden gate.

The sound worked like a lever to raise the grazing mustangs' heads. They all came up at once and stared at her.

"Nothing's wrong," Sam told the horses. "I'm just out on a wild goose chase."

Then she smiled to herself. Correction: a wild *horse* chase.

She had to start thinking like a horse. Now.

Sam closed her eyes to pretend she had four long legs and a tail that brushed the ground.

You're a horse, she told herself. It's been a long, hot day. Finally, the sun's gone down. The earth is cooling beneath your hooves. It's night and you can move about more freely. What do you do next?

Eat? Always.

Sleep? No, she'd feel frisky after dozing in brushy ravines during the heat of the day.

Drink? Yes!

That was it. Most times she'd seen the Phantom had been at the La Charla River as he led his herd to drink. But the La Charla was behind her and Pirate had been looking in the opposite direction.

The hot springs?

Sam turned the idea over again in her mind. Maybe. She'd have to ask Brynna if wild horses drank warm water. Until she could, she'd head in that direction.

The smell of burned grass was bitter even to Sam's human nostrils as she neared the rangeland scorched by the lightning-strike fire. Could the Phantom smell this peach over the black stench?

Something scurried nearby, but Sam didn't see it. It might have been a mouse or a night bird leading her away from its nest. Sam kept walking, rolling the velvety fruit between her palms.

Wait, what about the pit? Sure, the stallion's strong teeth could crush it, but she could accomplish two things at once if she took it out.

Cupping the peach in both hands, Sam bit through the skin, pushed her teeth toward the pit, then used her fingers to grab it and pull it out.

Now the sweet aroma should be strong enough for a horse to smell.

When he didn't magically appear, she kept walk-ing. She wasn't sleepy, anyway, so she'd search a little longer.

Ahead, Sam saw a pale mesa so smooth and curved,

it didn't seem to be made of rock and dirt. Instead of being hardened by centuries of weather, it looked like it had been sculpted from ice cream, then flattened on top and scooped smooth on each side.

Scalloped black wings tumbled toward Sam, then veered away and vanished. A bat searching for a bug dinner, she thought.

The howling hadn't come again for some time. She heard nothing but her own footfalls, but she kept feeling as if she were being followed.

Sam looked back over her shoulder. She'd walked a long way from Deerpath Ranch and there was no porch light to guide her back. She hoped Mrs. Allen wasn't a restless sleeper like Gram. If Mrs. Allen came outside and found the empty hammock, chaos would follow. She'd call out the sheriff's mounted patrol, every cowboy in the county, and the volunteer fire department.

Sam winced. How would she explain she'd come wandering out here on the advice of a horse? A hallucinating horse.

She really should start back, but Sam stalled. She stared up into the night sky, looking for more bats. She saw a pair of darting birds that Gram called nighthawks and Dallas called goat suckers.

Her eyes picked out the Big Dipper and she'd just about located Orion when a neigh floated over the blackened fields.

Yes! That raspy call had come from an adult

horse, probably a stallion.

A whinny answered from the ranch. Without meaning to, Sam gazed back over her shoulder, sighing in sympathy for Pirate.

*Poor baby,* she thought.

When she turned back, a blue-white form had materialized just yards away.

The Phantom stood in the charred field, legs braced and head lowered. Like an otherworldly beast ready to charge, his muscled shoulders swelled.

She knew it was the Phantom, though his fine-boned face and intelligent eyes were hidden by his overlong forelock. One front hoof struck over and over, as if he hated the ashy smell.

*Come to me, beauty,* Sam thought as the stallion stalked a few steps nearer. But then he leaped toward her.

Head level, ears flattened into a mane blown back by his lunge, the stallion's body bridged half the distance between them.

It's a mock charge. A play threat. It had to be. But as he came closer, the ground beneath Sam shuddered.

"'You know me, Zanzibar,'" Sam's words were half whisper, half gasp, and way too late.

Moonlight glinted pewter on his mane, silver on his back, white on the tail held straight out and fluttering as the stallion flashed by on her right. The warmth from his body passed her, circled behind her, and then he slid to a sand-spitting stop a few yards to her left.

A chuckling nicker came from the stallion and Sam felt weak and deflated.

"You like scaring me?" she asked.

Looking past her, the stallion blew through his lips. "You're bored?"

Who would believe she stood out here on the open range in shorts and sneakers, joking with a wild horse in the moonlight?

Would he come to her? Would he let her ride him? Or even touch him?

Sam's fingers ached to skim over the sterling spots glimmering beneath the stallion's dusty hide.

She tried not to move, keeping even her breaths small and shallow, letting him remember he was safe.

The Phantom remembered. Just like anyone's spoiled pet, he reached his lips toward her, seeking the peach.

Sam's heart flew up, but she made the moment last. The stallion's soft nose pushed at her fingers as she wondered how many humans had made friends with wild horses.

Not many. A Native American shaman, probably. A Celtic maiden worshipped as a goddess for her power to lure wild things. And Samantha Forster, who was too foolhardy for her own good. But look what it had earned her.

"Ow! Careful!" Sam yelped.

The stallion wanted the peach and he wasn't feeling patient. Sam flattened her palm and let him take it.

"It's my own fault," she confessed.

Bobbing his head, chewing, and strewing bits of peach and saliva, the Phantom gave her a side glance that said he'd never considered any other possibility. Sam kept her lips closed over a giggle. The stallion was so full of himself. She loved him for his royal attitude and she didn't care that he'd splattered her with his snack.

Some girls might have shrunk away squealing, but she treasured the moment when he treated her like one of his herd.

Besides, she was creeping closer, scooting the soles of her sneakers ever nearer, without lifting her feet for a step.

The stallion wasn't fooled or frightened when she grabbed a handful of his mane.

Before she could gather herself to swing up and mount, he simply sidestepped out of reach.

Amazed she didn't fall and didn't lose her grip on his ropy mane, Sam crooned to the horse, "C'mon, boy, I'd never hurt you."

Peach juice dripped from his mouth. He considered her plea for a minute and walked away, but he didn't shake her hand from his mane, just towed her along with him.

It was better than nothing, so Sam trotted to keep up.

"Where're we going, big boy? Hmm?"

Lengthening his stride, he moved faster and Sam feared he'd break into a trot and leave her behind.

"Now or never," she muttered and, hopping on one foot, she threw herself at the stallion, aiming for the glowing spot of moonlight on his back.

## Chapter Twelve

*T*he Phantom bolted.

Sam's aim hadn't taken his sudden rush into account. Her lips grazed his withers just before a hind hoof came down on her tennis-shoed toes.

Her yelp of pain must have sounded playful to the stallion, because he ducked his head and frolicked a few strides before swiveling a kick toward the stars. Instinctively, Sam raised her arms to shield herself from his lashing hooves, but she'd only stumbled, not fallen. As the stallion trotted on, she followed him.

"I'm going with you," she told him, but he headed toward a stand of tall weeds, crashed through them, and disappeared.

Splash!

She heard it and knew she'd been right. The stallion had been headed for the hot springs when he'd come upon her.

Favoring her right foot and wondering just how much the stallion weighed, Sam ran clumsily after him. This was no time for moaning and babying herself. She could look at her smashed toes later. Now she had a chance to ride the Phantom.

She'd mounted him for the first time in the river. Could he be reminding her how to do it right?

Ahead of her was a stand of reeds, not weeds. Tall and supple, they surrounded the hot springs then gave way to lower plants and the pool itself.

The stallion stood on the opposite side of the hot springs, drinking. Sam could hear him, but the shade from the reeds made him just a pale shape. She couldn't see the angle of his ears or the expression in his eyes.

But he'd been playful just a second ago, so she approached, walking slowly around the rim of the hot springs.

"Don't you need a bath, boy?" Sam coaxed. "If you go in, I'll come with you."

Jake had told her years ago that the point of water training was safety. Neither horse nor rider could be easily injured.

Looking across the mist that danced above the hot springs, Sam thought there'd be another benefit:

tranquility. She imagined the warm water lapping around them as she sat astride the stallion.

"You need to cooperate," she told him.

Slowly, regally, the stallion raised his head from the water.

"Well, you don't exactly need to," Sam said, since she didn't dare give him anything that sounded like an order.

Sam caught a flicker of white as the Phantom's eyes rolled toward the reeds.

"You're okay. You're not surrounded," Sam assured him.

But the stallion seemed certain he was. Even though he could easily brush past the cattails and water grasses, Sam was crowding him. His tail swished and he sucked in a suspicious draft of air.

He flinched as she touched his mane. She weaved her fingers through the strong strands, but they nearly cut her fingers as he surged away.

"You're telling me no, aren't you?" Sam asked mournfully. She wanted to ride him so much. "Will it ever happen again?"

The Phantom's wariness only increased. His neck jerked up so suddenly, she had to release her grip on his mane, and then he was backing. Three steps, four, and his ears flattened in anger.

"I'm sorry," Sam said, but the stallion's glare wasn't for her.

He stared over her head, past the rocks that

sheltered the hot springs. He couldn't see through them, but he must have sensed something, because he was leaving, his mighty chest shoving through the reeds on the far side of the hot springs.

Sam sighed as she heard his hooves clatter on stone and cross hard-packed earth. No galloping strides shook the ground beneath her, but the night felt desolate. The Phantom had gone and she stood in the desert, alone.

Limping and biting her lip, Sam stared at the moon-washed ground before her as she made her way back to the ranch. Suddenly she was exhausted. It was two o'clock in the morning and she felt as if all her energy had been drained away.

What had she done wrong? She was pretty sure he hadn't been reacting to her bossiness. The Phantom's ego just let her orders bounce off.

No, he'd been alert to some noise or smell she couldn't sense.

And then she heard something, too. A scuffing sound she almost recognized made her look up.

A figure slumped against the fence of the mustang pasture. Ice-blond hair and the glimmer of metal crutches told her it was Gabe.

Her heart thudded so hard, she wondered if it actually struck her breastbone. She and the silver stallion hadn't been alone.

But . . . Sam released a sigh of relief. She'd

walked a couple of miles in the last hour. He couldn't have followed her. Terrible as the thought was, she was glad Gabe couldn't have kept up.

"What are you doing here?" Sam asked. She tried to sound casual, as if teenage cowgirls always strolled around in the middle of the night.

He didn't answer until she stopped right next to him. When she did, Sam knew something was wrong.

"Spying on you, I guess," Gabe said. He touched the binoculars around his neck.

Sam felt as if someone had grabbed her ankles and cracked her entire body like a whip. She drooped against the pasture fence.

She'd hidden her friendship with the stallion so well, for so long . . .

Her nose and fingers felt cold. Black dots frenzied in front of her eyes, crowding out the sight of the awful boy.

Is this what it felt like when you were about to faint?

"So that's the horse you told me about on the phone," Gabe said.

What should she do? What should she say? Was there any point in denying it?

"Yes."

"The wild horse you're friends with." He pressed her to go on.

"Yes." Her lips felt numb, but she blinked and she could see more clearly.

"So, is he wild or tame?"

Sam stared at Gabe. She didn't know what to say. Even if she had the right words, she didn't know if she could pronounce them. She felt weird and disconnected.

"Look," he snapped. "I couldn't see that much. You kept going past rocks and it's really dark and then you went through that high foresty part. Quit holding your head like that. You're freaking me out."

Until then, Sam hadn't realized the heels of her hands were pressed against her temples and her fingers were buried in her hair. She dropped her hands to her sides and shook them, trying to get blood pulsing back through her fingers.

"You really surprised me," she said, finally.

Once she sounded normal, Gabe's expression made an ugly change.

"You're not just surprised, either," he said. "I bet you're feeling totally guilty for matching the crippled kid with the wrecked horse." He tilted his weight toward one crutch as he jerked a thumb back toward the ranch yard and Pirate. "While you have that really outstanding one."

*Wrecked* horse? Sam pictured Pirate splashing in the lake at War Drum Flats, running across the *playa*, and protecting the little roan filly from Linc Slocum's feral dogs.

"What did you say?" she hissed.

"You heard me," Gabe sneered. "You and my grandma thought it would be cute or helpful or—

whatever—to pair up the two losers."

Sam could hear herself panting for breath.

*I'm hyperventilating,* she thought, but not from surprise or shock. She was wrestling for control of herself. She didn't want to do the unforgivable. Not that she could imagine what that would be.

This guy deserved whatever she could dish out, Sam thought, but she'd be in big trouble if she strangled him.

Shoulders squared, chin up, and green eyes narrowed, Gabe looked like a guy who'd just thrown down a dare. While he waited for her to pick it up, Sam thought of Jake.

The Ely brothers had been known to fight—both each other and other guys. Though they were punished thoroughly for it, they still had a reputation as brawlers and Darrell, one of Jake's best friends, had tipped Sam off, so she'd know when one of them was truly mad.

*These Elys get quieter and quieter, the more they're riled,* Darrell had told her. *Long about the time they're quiet as a stone wall, that's when you'd better take off runnin'.*

It sounded like a good strategy to Sam.

Instead of yelling and trying to shake some sense into Gabe, she lowered her voice and spoke softly.

"That colt," she said, "is no loser."

"I notice you don't include me," he said sarcastically.

"That's because this has nothing to do with you. Your grandmother"—Sam paused and raised both hands in frustration—"might not agree. And if letting you help is the price I have to pay to give that colt a place to stay this week, then I'll put up with you. But I'm here to help *him* and you'd better stay out of my way while I do it."

As soon as she'd uttered them, the words echoed in Sam's mind. She would be kicked off this ranch for sure if Mrs. Allen heard about this conversation.

But Gabe wasn't done fighting. He leaned toward her as if he had something more vicious to say.

"You think anyone's going to want him with those burns?"

Sam closed her eyes for a second. Gabe must be taking out his own unhappiness on her. The HARP girls had taught her that that happened a lot, but how could he be so mean?

Sam wet her lips. She wanted to give herself time to calm down, but since that probably would have taken until January, she did her best.

"Those burns already look better. They're pink and blistered in places where they looked like . . ." Sam searched for words to describe Pirate's face on that awful day. "Bubbles of charcoal," she said finally.

"I still say—"

"I don't care what you say," Sam told him in a level voice. "If you could have seen that colt, running across the range, leading all the other young mustangs—" Sam's voice broke. She was too close to crying to continue.

"Yeah, and if you could have seen *me* before—"

Gabe's mouth pulled into a deep frown. Then, he threw both his crutches down into the dirt.

Neither of them could help staring at the fallen crutches.

Shocked by what Gabe had done, Sam almost bent to pick them up. Didn't he need those crutches to walk?

Sam knew she was in way over her head.

What would Gabe do next? Was this like, some kind of symbolic gesture? Was he so afraid he *would* need them, forever, that he was trying to throw them away?

Sam didn't know.

All she knew was that Gabe should be talking with an expert, someone who understood what he was going through.

But right now, in the middle of the night, he only had her.

She was still angry. She hated what he'd said about Pirate, but something kept coming back to her.

*You don't punish fear.*

Gabe was definitely afraid.

But wait. Dr. Scott had said that about the colt. Well shoot, Sam thought, maybe horse psychology was all she had to go on.

Gabe leaned rigid and defiant against the pasture fence.

No, she wouldn't pick up those crutches and help

him settle between their support. She'd bet almost anything that Gabe would rather spend all night out here than accept her help.

"You still say this has nothing to do with me?" Gabe demanded, but Sam heard a plea under the meanness.

"Yeah, I do," Sam told him. "This time next month, you probably won't need those." Sam nodded at the fallen crutches. "This time next month, if he keeps having his crazy episodes, they'll decide it's more merciful to put that colt down."

Gabe leaned the back of his head against the fence and looked up into the night sky.

"I came here to get away from trouble," he said. Then he gave a short laugh. "Actually, I wanted to get away from my friends feeling sorry for me. I guess you've got that no-pity part handled."

Sam laughed, too, but she really hoped he didn't tell Mrs. Allen about all this. She put her hand on Gabe's arm, carefully.

"Look, you're not going to be here for long, and I really could use you as a spotter when I start working with the colt tomorrow. It won't kill you to think about something besides yourself for just a few days, right?"

"It might even help," he said sarcastically.

"Well, it might," she insisted. "But don't forget—"

"I know. You're here for the horse."

"Absolutely, and I'm going back to sleep next to

his corral, right now." Sam took a few steps away, worried about those crutches, but trying not to show it. "Good night."

She didn't look back. She listened. She didn't hear anything. He was clearly waiting until she was out of sight before he tried to get them and make it back to the house.

She'd given up hearing anything at all from him, when he called after her.

"Hey, Sam, were you trying to get on that wild horse?"

Oh my gosh, there went her thudding heart again. But he couldn't have seen her very clearly if he was asking. And a lot depended on this. The Phantom could be in danger if anyone discovered their bond was so strong, she could actually ride him.

So Sam decided to lie.

She turned around, hands on hips.

"No, Gabe, I didn't try to get on him." She shook her head, as if he weren't very smart. "That stallion tried to bite me and I was shoving him away."

"That's what I thought," Gabe said, and his voice trailed away.

The horses barely stirred as Sam finally got her shoes untied, then climbed back into the hammock. But this time, it wasn't the horses she worried about. Sam lay on her side, staring at the glowing numbers on her watch. Five minutes had passed since she'd left Gabe down by the wild horse pasture. Ten minutes. Eleven. At last, thirteen minutes later, she heard the plop-scuff of Gabe planting his crutch tips, then swinging up to them.

Sam released the breath she'd been holding and realized her hands had been fisted, too.

As her eyes closed, Sam heard the rusty hinges creak. Plop-scuff. Gabe moved down the garden path to the front door. It didn't take long for him to get it open.

The dogs must have been asleep, because their staccato barks were halfhearted. So was Gabe's grumble.

"Get out of my way, you little creeps," he told Imp and Angel.

And from what Sam could hear, they did.

## *Chapter Thirteen*

Sam's first thought as she wakened was that she must be camping.

Campfire smoke had swirled through her dreams and she wasn't sleeping in her own bed, that was for sure.

Then, she realized it was daybreak at Deerpath Ranch. Her back sagged with the curve of a hammock and her legs were bent at the knees, folded to one side. The twinge in her toes brought a smile and a warm feeling as she remembered the Phantom's wild majesty, but her next morning thought made her groan.

*You'd better stay out of my way . . . Would it kill you to think about somebody else?*

Sam opened her eyes and stared at the blue bowl of sky overhead, wishing it would fall. Why had she said those things last night? She was basically a nice person, but no one who'd been listening to her last night would believe it. And there was no way to unsay words you'd blurted out, no matter how sorry you were.

"I am definitely getting kicked off this ranch," Sam moaned.

A horse snorted and hooves skittered as Sam sat up.

Since Calico, Ginger, and Judge were just looking forlornly into their feed bins, Sam was pretty sure it had been the colt who'd stood close enough to her hammock to be disturbed by her movement.

"Hi, sweet pony," Sam said, then clucked to the colt.

He faced away from her, black tail swishing. This was a change. He'd decided she wasn't dangerous. He could turn his back on her and she probably wouldn't leap on him like a predator.

This was progress, but the wrong kind. Sam watched the colt sidle closer to the old saddle horses. She and Dr. Scott had made a mistake. They'd felt sorry for the colt because he'd been separated from his herd, but as long as he had a herd, why should he bond with her?

"Calico, Ginger, Judge," Sam called to the horses. They raised their heads, then swung them hopefully toward the barn and feed room. "If Mrs. Allen says it's okay, it's moving day for you three."

Sam's stomach growled, but she fed the horses first and gave them fresh water.

As she added strawberry-kiwi Kool-Aid to Pirate's bucket, she noticed the colt watching. He blinked the white eyelashes of one eye and the sandy red ones on the other. It seemed to Sam that there was a rebuke in his expression.

"Don't worry," she said quietly. "I know I'm not the one who usually does this. But it's you and me, now, good boy. Dr. Scott isn't here. I'm sorry."

Once the horses were cared for, Sam hurried to Mrs. Allen's house.

Click click. Pant pant. Snuffle snuffle.

Sam heard Imp and Angel at the door before she opened it. Once she was inside, the dogs' flat little faces pressed against Sam's legs and they slobbered on her shins.

"Nice to see you, too," she said, making her way into the quiet kitchen.

Even though it was already seven o'clock, no one, except the dogs, was awake. Mrs. Allen wasn't an early riser like Gram, or maybe she'd lain awake late last night, worrying over Gabe.

Sam poured herself a glass of milk and drank it while nibbling a granola bar from the box Mrs. Allen had brought with yesterday's groceries. She also thought about moving Mrs. Allen's saddle horses.

She should ask permission, but she only had a few days with Pirate and, as Dallas had said one morning on the cattle drive, they were "burnin' daylight."

Sam threw each of the panting Boston bulldogs a piece of her granola bar, then wadded up the wrapper and threw it away.

"The worst thing that can happen," she told the chewing dogs, "if I move the horses and she doesn't want them in with the mustangs, is that she'll make me move them back. Right?" she asked, but the dogs just gazed up at her, licking their lips.

Finding Calico's bridle and slipping it on the pinto mare was easy. The tricky part was releasing the three older horses while keeping the colt penned.

He neighed frantically and darted randomly toward the gate and away from it, unsure whether he was more afraid of Sam or of being left alone.

"This will all work out in the end," she promised the colt.

The two pintos and the old bay milled around until Sam snagged Calico's reins and led her to a rock to mount.

She hadn't ridden barefooted, in shorts, for a long time. She'd done it all the time as a little kid, but now Sam felt wobbly and unbalanced.

She clucked her tongue and started herding the horses toward the mustang pasture. It would be easier if someone had gone on ahead to open the gate, but she hoped the captive mustangs would shy away from all the activity long enough that she could open the gate and herd the saddle horses through without any wild horses escaping.

Inconsolable at being abandoned, Pirate neighed and raced along the fence. Back and forth he galloped, crying to the other horses to come back.

Hardening her heart, Sam told herself this was for his own good.

And what about the way she'd talked to Gabe last night? Had that been for his own good, too?

Sam tried to remember everything she knew about Gabe. Early in his hospitalization, Mrs. Allen had told Sam that Gabe shifted between being angry and so sad, it broke her heart. She mentioned that he regretted taking his legs for granted and listed things he thought he'd miss, like skateboarding, kicking a soccer ball, and running to class when he was tardy.

She remembered, again, that during their one phone call, she'd asked Gabe "What's up?" and he'd answered, "Not me." Although she'd felt stupid and insensitive at the time, now she could see that Gabe's dark humor could help him get through this. Besides, she'd said lots worse things to him last night.

Whinnying wildly, taking snorting breaths in-between, Pirate continued to beg the other horses to come back.

"No one is going to sleep through this," Sam told Calico.

Just then, Sam heard the squawk of the rusty gate. She glanced back over her shoulder in time to see Gabe making his way toward her.

Wait. Her breath caught for a minute. No, she was probably imagining it, probably just wishing it were true, but it looked as if he was putting more weight on his uncast leg.

It could be true, but it might not mean anything, either. Yesterday Gabe had mentioned he had limited mobility in that leg. The other leg was shattered, and hadn't he said something about having a metal rod in it? But what did "limited mobility" mean? Was it okay for him to be putting more weight on that leg?

"What are you doing?" Gabe called after her now.

"Putting them in the other pasture so that I can work with the colt," she said. Sam bit her lip. Gabe was following her anyway. Why shouldn't she ask for his help? "Want to open that gate for me?"

She'd almost asked, Can you open that gate? but a flicker of understanding told her to let him decide. There was a second of hesitation while he made up his mind. Then Gabe said, "Sure."

Sweat beaded his upper lip by the time he managed to open the bolt, avoid the jostling horses, and keep his crutches pressed under his arms.

"Thanks," Sam said as she slipped off Calico's bridle and gave the old mare a pat on the rump so she'd move off with the other horses.

Sam slipped through the gate and shot the bolt

home, then turned to Gabe. "It was a lot easier with your help. Doing it alone, I might not have gotten them all through at once."

He nodded, looking thoughtful as he stared at the mustangs.

"I'm sorry that, last night—"

"Forget about it," Gabe told her.

"No, really . . ." She almost went on, but she caught a look in his eyes that she'd seen in Jake's and Dad's and Dallas'. He just didn't want to rehash an emotional scene, so Sam swallowed her apology and told him about the captive mustangs.

Mrs. Allen had told him how she'd come to own the horses, but he'd never seen them before.

"That big liver chestnut—"

"And by that you mean 'brown'?" Gabe asked.

"Well, yeah, dark brown. The one strutting over there is Roman. He thinks he's the boss. I don't see Belle and Faith, but see that black mare with the bright bay colt?"

"And by *bay* you mean brown?" Gabe teased again.

"A totally different shade of brown," Sam insisted. "But, yeah. Those two are named Licorice and Windfall. That yellow dun," Sam said, pointing, then added, "yellow, not brown, see her?—is named Fourteen and I don't know if her baby has a name yet."

"*He* doesn't have a name." Gabe's voice was flat.

"How come?"

"The colt?" Sam asked, but Gabe shook his head.

Could he mean the Phantom? Was he thinking of what he'd seen last night? But then Gabe clarified what he meant by jerking his head back toward the ranch yard.

"Oh. Him?" Sam gave herself time to think. Pirate's wasn't a secret name like the Phantom's or Tempest's. The colt had never heard it whispered, and yet she was reluctant to share it. "No. Dr. Scott and I just figured it would be less confusing if we let his new owner choose a name."

Gabe's lips shifted sideways. He looked kind of disgusted.

"What?" Sam asked.

"Doesn't it . . . not that I care. I mean, it's not like he knows the other horses have names and he doesn't. It's just . . . it seems . . ." He shook his head. "Man, I need to wake up. I can't even talk this morning."

Sam wasn't about to let him off the hook so easily. "Seems like what?"

"Like if he *mattered*, he'd have a name."

"Give him one," Sam suggested. The words popped out of her mouth before she thought about them.

"No way. He's not my horse. Do I *look* like a cowboy?"

"It was just an idea," Sam said. "But hey, I've got to get to work with him. We only have a few days. Have you eaten breakfast yet?"

"I skipped it," Gabe said. "It's not like I'm doing anything."

"You're joking, right?" Sam asked. She looked at his forearms, tense with muscles where he gripped his crutches.

A trace of yesterday's cockiness crossed his face, but Gabe just shrugged. In fact, Sam thought he made kind of a big deal of that shrug, as if he were flexing those muscles, too.

"So, are you just checking on my nutrition, or what?" he asked.

Sam shook her head. "I have to put the zinc oxide on the colt's face and I'm not sure if he'll let me."

"The vet just said do it."

"I know," Sam said, puzzled. "But I don't think he's going to just stand still while I try it the first time," Sam said. "And even though he's got a halter on, he's a big strong colt. I need a spotter."

"What do you think I'm going to do if he tries to trample you?" Gabe demanded.

"Yell," Sam said.

"Yell? Like 'Shoo, you bad horsy'?"

"That ought to do it," Sam said. "He's still pretty spooky and, really, except for movie horses and stallions whose mares are threatened, horses don't really charge that much."

Sam tried to keep a smile from playing on her lips as she remembered the Phantom's mock charge last night.

She wasn't sure whether Gabe saw her expression or not. When Sam looked at him, leaning against the fence and rolling the tension from his shoulder, Gabe said, "He doesn't look anything like that white stallion, does he?"

"Yeah he does," Sam said firmly.

"Naw," Gabe insisted, but his green eyes narrowed, studying the colt as if he hoped she was right.

So, even though there was no way to be certain, Sam said, "They're father and son."

"Wow," Gabe said.

This time Sam couldn't smother her smile. She wished Gabe hadn't seen her with the Phantom, but it had given him a better of idea of the wildness Pirate had left behind.

## *Chapter Fourteen*

"How long is this supposed to take?" Gabe asked.

For an hour, Sam had been trying to get close enough to touch the colt. The sun had risen above the horizon and Gabe pulled at the neck of his long-sleeved T-shirt.

"It depends," Sam said. She kept walking after the colt, letting him think she was talking to him as they continued their dance of stop and watch, advance and retreat. She was closer than she'd been all morning when he bolted away. Again. "This could go on for days, but I don't think it will."

"Days?" Gabe asked. "Why?"

"All herd animals—pack animals, too, I think, like

dogs—are looking for a leader. You just have to prove you're the right one for the job. Some horses are harder to convince than others."

"Yeah? So how do they tell if you're the right one?" Gabe sounded sarcastic.

Sam wasn't surprised that Gabe sounded skeptical. Dallas, River Bend's foreman, still resisted these ideas, too, and he'd worked with horses his entire life.

"Some people say that in the wild, the lead horse is the one that can make other horses move," Sam said. She was picturing the Phantom herding his mares and thinking of Queen, who'd been his lead mare, until she noticed Pirate paid closer attention to her when Gabe was directly behind her. "Hmm."

"What?" Gabe said, batting at the wave of dust the colt had raised as he bolted away. Gabe coughed, then muttered something about someone burning off nearby fields before he made a rolling gesture with his hand, so she'd keep explaining.

"I think it makes more sense, that a horse obeys a human if he—the horse, that is—doesn't get scared or hurt trying to do what that human asks him to do," Sam said.

"Like a good coach," Gabe said.

Sam hadn't been sure Gabe really cared, but at least he was paying attention.

"This guy," Sam said, and when she pointed at Pirate, he began circling the pen at a trot, "wasn't very high in his herd hierarchy, so what Dr. Scott said, about him being almost halter broken, makes sense.

"But Dark Sunshine, a buckskin mustang who's sort of mine, not only spent some time with the Phantom as a lead mare, but she's had some bad treatment by humans. She barely trusts anyone, and she's not completely halter broken even now."

"How long have you had her?" Gabe asked in a dreading tone.

"About a year," Sam said, but she ignored Gabe's groan, because she'd just seen what she was waiting for.

The colt stopped. His shoulders, neck, and head loosened and he walked a few steps in her direction.

"That's my good boy," Sam crooned.

Quick as she could, she opened the tube of zinc oxide and let the colt catch the familiar scent. Instead of trying to grab his halter and confine him, she inched up to the young horse and lightly covered his burns with the cream.

He trembled at her touch and his legs shook, ready to carry him away, but he stood long enough that she finished. Then she stepped back. The colt did the same, bobbing his head.

"That's it for now," Sam said. "You were a good boy."

"Why not keep going? Clip on that lead rope thing?" Gabe whispered. "You had him doing exactly what you wanted."

Sam opened the gate, slipped through, and stood beside Gabe.

"He's a baby," Sam said. "And I wouldn't have worked him as long as I did if I hadn't had to get that sunscreen on him for his own good. Besides, it's always best to stop when the horse has done something right, not when you give up in frustration."

"Makes sense," Gabe said.

They both turned, then, at the sound of the wrought-iron gate.

"Do you think that just needs oil?" Gabe asked.

"I have no idea, but it looks like your grandmother's delivering breakfast."

Sam was right. Mrs. Allen carried a pink plastic bowl that held little silver pouches, napkins, and paper cups full of orange juice.

"Breakfast burritos," she announced. "Formerly frozen and not nearly as good as what Grace would whip up," Mrs. Allen said to Sam.

"They're delicious," Sam said, chewing the first spicy bite. "I didn't know I was so hungry."

At first Sam thought Mrs. Allen was frowning because a stiff breeze threatened to snatch the paper napkins away. But then Sam noticed that though she'd finished nearly half of the burrito and most of her juice, Gabe's burrito and juice still sat on the tray.

Of course he couldn't hold himself upright and eat and drink at the same time, Sam thought. The complications just kept coming.

"Gabe," Mrs. Allen said. "Let me help you."

"Thanks, but I'm not hungry." His voice was tight. Still, Sam noticed he wasn't looking at the tray, but at the colt.

Pirate's knees buckled, though his head was raised and his eyes rolled white.

"Oh my heavens, what's wrong?" Mrs. Allen asked.

The colt's red coat had turned dark along his flanks.

Sweat, Sam thought. She'd seen this before.

"He has these—spells."

"I know that's what Brynna said," Mrs. Allen sounded worried, as if this looked worse than what she'd expected.

Pirate's knees straightened. His mane lifted on a hot wind and his nostrils flared, closed, and flared again. His lips moved anxiously as if he would tell them what was wrong.

Froth gathered in the corners of his mouth. He took a few stuttering steps, then staggered.

"He's scared to death," Gabe barely choked the words out.

He was right.

Panic overwhelmed the colt, sending him bolting into the fence. When it held under his assault, he swerved, hooves scrabbling for traction and failing because of the sharpness of his turn.

He slammed flat down on his side. His slender

legs flailed, determined to rise and escape whatever terrified him. He lurched upright and his ears flopped, one back, the other to the side.

"He's not supposed to overheat. Where's the hose?" Gabe asked his grandmother. She pointed, and he looked at Sam. "We're supposed to wet him down."

Sam started toward the hose. She turned the water on and the sudden splattering caught the colt's attention.

"Wait," Sam said. "I think —"

The colt's shaking slowed to a quiver. He swung his head from side to side as if shuddering from the touch of cobwebs.

He stared at the water and his heaving breaths quieted.

"Mrs. Allen, can I have this?" Sam reached for the plastic bowl without taking her eyes from the colt.

"Of course." Mrs. Allen grabbed everything from the bowl and held it steady while Sam filled it with water.

"The scraper's still in that box," Gabe said. "And the sponge. Is that what you're going to do? Sponge down those big veins the vet talked about?"

"If he'll let me," Sam said. She gathered the sponge and bowl and returned to the corral.

The colt shied and paced to the far side of the corral, then loosed a worried neigh to the other horses.

"If he doesn't knock this off in a minute, I say we squirt him down," Gabe said, and it was clear to Sam that he wasn't angry. He was worried.

Then, as they both watched, the horse's skin shivered. He shook his head, making his black mane dance, then seemed to relax.

"So that's what you and Dr. Scott meant by *loco*," Gabe said.

"That's it, but he's okay now," Sam said in a singsong voice. "My big boy's just fine, isn't he?"

Again, Sam noticed the colt focused on her best when she passed near Gabe. For some reason Pirate was more interested in him than her. So she stood in front of Gabe, babbling nonsense, until the colt allowed her to squeeze the sponge over his neck and legs, letting the water dribble down and cool him. When he nipped at the scrapers, Sam used her hands to rub the excess water off his coat.

"Now walk him around," Gabe ordered.

"Well, I know that's what the vet said." Sam tried not to sound impatient. "But it's not that easy. I'd have to get a lead rope on him and convince him to follow me. Just give me a minute."

Impatient and clearly worried, Gabe moved closer to Mrs. Allen.

Although Pirate's hind hooves stayed planted, his front hooves tracked Gabe's movements.

"Do that again," Sam said. When Gabe didn't respond, she decided bossing him around wasn't the best approach. "I'm sorry to ask, but please move someplace else along the fence line. I don't know why, but—" Sam broke off, shaking her head.

Gabe didn't wait for an explanation. Using his shirt sleeve to rub perspiration from his face, Gabe winced as if his arms ached, then moved a few yards along the corral fence.

"He's following you," Sam said.

"My goodness," Mrs. Allen said. "He is."

"It's a coincidence," Gabe said.

His own grandmother ignored him. "Do you think it's because he's only been around Dr. Scott, and they're both men?" she asked.

"You're *both* nuts," Gabe said, but Sam thought he was flattered by the colt's attention.

"He's definitely following you, but I don't know why," Sam said.

Sam didn't care, either. She just knew that this was going to make taming the colt a whole lot easier.

After spending an entire day as the colt's sole focus, Sam thought Gabe would be happy. When Dad and Brynna had called the previous night, she'd told them everything was fine. Dr. Scott had also called, to see how the colt was coming along, and she'd told him that the colt thought Gabe was fascinating and they were both happy.

But Gabe wasn't.

The next morning, she was adding Kool-Aid to the colt's water when Gabe made his way past the rusty iron gate to stand beside her at the corral.

Gabe didn't say anything at first, just tapped his fingers on the crossbars of his crutches. He kept doing it until Sam looked at him out of the corner of her eye.

"My friend Luis just called," Gabe told her, but he didn't quit tapping.

"Great!" Sam said, but then she met Gabe's green eyes. "Not great?"

Gabe shrugged, and then he kind of swayed between the two crutches. Sam got the impression he'd be tapping his foot if he could.

"What did he say?" she asked him.

Gabe shrugged. And started tapping his fingers again.

Sam finished filling the water bucket and gathered an armload of hay for the mustang. When Gabe figured out she wasn't going to beg for details, he finally told her about his talk with Luis.

"He and Yogi are going to help coach a little kids' soccer team and they want to know if I can do one third of the practices."

To Sam, this sounded like good news.

"You can, can't you?" Sam asked.

"I'm going to miss this entire soccer season," Gabe said.

"But these are—what? Elementary school kids? You know enough to coach them without playing this season, right?"

"Of course, but the thing is, I'm a forward. Even

if my legs come back all the way, it's going to take a long time until I can run like I used to."

Sam cast about for a comment that would cheer him up.

"I don't know that much about soccer, but could you be a goalie? I mean, they don't run as much, do they? And they throw a lot. You're building up a lot of strength in your arms."

Gabe started to say something, then stopped. For just a second, Sam saw a glimmer of pride in his eyes, but then it was gone. Gabe shook his head in disgust, as if no one could fill in the gaps in her knowledge of the game he loved.

When Gabe started tapping the crossbars on his crutches again, Sam wanted to reach over and grab his fingers, but the iron gate creaked and his grandmother saved him.

Mrs. Allen bustled across the ranch yard holding a leash in each hand. Imp and Angel strained ahead of her, headed for the orange truck. The two Boston bulldogs clearly weren't used to walking on leashes, and it suddenly came to Sam that Mrs. Allen was trying to keep the dogs from bounding around Gabe's ankles, as they surely would do unrestrained.

"I'm running into Alkali for milk," Mrs. Allen said. "I bought all those groceries the day before yesterday and forgot milk. Now we have only a cup or so left. I don't know what I was thinking. Will you kids stay safe while I'm gone?"

Mrs. Allen looked so pointedly at Sam—not Gabe—that Sam answered, "Sure."

"It's not like we're *going* anywhere," Gabe said.

Mrs. Allen's eyes and lips drooped. She looked so sad, Sam thought, but only for a second.

"Well, you're *going* to adjust your attitude while I'm gone," Mrs. Allen said. "I'm sure you don't remember this, but your grandfather had a perfect description of the way you acted when you were pouting."

Sam sucked in her breath. *Pouting* was one of those words a sixteen-year-old guy would probably resent.

"I'm not—" he snarled.

"He said you were squirmy as a worm in a bed of ants," she interrupted.

"That's disgusting!" Gabe said.

Sam thought of the twitching and tapping he'd been doing since he talked with Luis and decided it was actually a pretty good description. But she decided not to say so.

After Mrs. Allen drove away, Gabe and Sam didn't talk.

Together they stared at the mustang.

"I'd rather have something wrong with my face than my legs," Gabe said.

Sam shivered, but she kept looking at Pirate as she asked, "Are you sure? Your face is the first thing everyone notices about you."

"Like these crutches aren't that noticeable?" Gabe asked with a bitter laugh. "You could've fooled me. Sorry," he said, then. "It's not your fault and it's a waste of time to talk about it. No one's going to give me a choice."

Sam didn't know what to do. How could she help Gabe?

If he were a horse, she'd try something different to get the same point across. If he was sensitive to a certain kind of bit, for instance, she'd try a hackamore.

Could that work with him?

If he didn't like her suggestions or those from his grandmother, maybe she'd let the colt take over.

"Hey," Sam said. She dug into the box Dr. Scott had brought and pulled out the big rubber soccer ball. "I know where you can get some practice."

"What do you expect me to do? My legs don't work, remember?"

"Gabe, I'm not being mean. For some reason, that little horse has decided you're interesting. He needs a buddy and Dr. Scott said he loves that ball. What if you just went in there and batted it to him?"

"With my crutch?"

"Your crutch, your hand, your head—" Sam stopped, because she could see Gabe was tempted.

Then he glanced toward the house, even though Mrs. Allen was gone.

"Do I go inside the corral?" he asked.

"No." Sam shook her head so hard, she felt her

auburn hair whirl. "He's still wild, and even though he wouldn't mean to hurt you, I'm not sure." —Sam slowed her words, trying not to make him irritated all over again—"that you could get out of his way fast enough if he goes *loco* again. Besides, I think that would get your grandmother really mad."

"I don't care," Gabe said. "She's the one who said I had to work with him. And then she threatened to kick me out if I didn't."

Gabe shifted his weight on his crutches, then headed toward the corral gate briskly, as if taking up a challenge.

*Chapter Fifteen* ❧

Gabe didn't look up from playing soccer with the colt when Mrs. Allen returned from Alkali.

At the last second, Gabe had agreed to stay outside the corral. Since then, he'd spent an hour balancing on his uncasted leg, gripping the top fence rail with one hand as he hung head down to punch the ball with his crutch from under the last fence board. Because the horse toy was egg-shaped, the ball rolled unpredictably and Gabe made his way from one side of the pen to the other and back again dozens of times.

"It's less like soccer and more like playing pool with a jumping bean," Gabe said. His face was flushed, but in a good way, Sam thought, and the colt definitely enjoyed his contortions.

Gabe didn't seem to care that the colt rarely used his teeth to grab the ball's handle and shake it, and that he'd only kicked it once and trotted after it three or four times. It seemed enough to the boy that Pirate was playing with him.

Sam couldn't have explained why the scene satisfied her so, but it did. The two seemed right together. Gabe didn't demand more of the mustang than he gave freely, and even when he didn't react to the rolling ball, Pirate filled his eyes with Gabe.

"That's sappy," Gabe protested when Sam told him.

"But true. He thinks you're really interesting."

Gabe shrugged, but he let her words stand as his grandmother came huffing from the truck.

"That danged Slocum," Mrs. Allen snapped as she was towed along by the small black-and-white dogs. "I saw him in the cafe with his daughter—who's really an awfully pretty girl, even if she does come from bad bloodlines—and I told him what I thought about him choosing now, when this colt is in such a delicate condition, to be burning off his fields. That hardhearted son of a gun didn't care. And what's more, he doesn't plan to stop."

Sam felt as if Mrs. Allen had snapped her fingers to bring her out of a trance.

"What?" Sam said.

"Try to listen, Samantha," Mrs. Allen said briskly.

"Before I picked up our milk, I stopped at Clara's for a cup of coffee and maybe a little pie, I can't exactly remember, I was so upset."

"Who is this guy, Grandma?" Gabe demanded. "What did he say to you?"

Although Gabe wasn't flexing and vowing to beat up the guy who'd annoyed his grandmother, Sam imagined his blond hair got bristlier and his pale eyebrows dropped in a threatening way.

She couldn't help thinking it would be fun to see him take on Linc Slocum.

Mrs. Allen said, sighing, "I don't know why I'm even surprised. The man is so self-centered — although his daughter Rachel did mention she'd heard I had a houseguest who was quite an accomplished athlete, and wondered if she might visit." Mrs. Allen smiled meaningfully at Gabe.

He rolled his eyes at Mrs. Allen's obvious matchmaking.

"I hope you told her 'no,'" Sam blurted.

"Why, Samantha!" Mrs. Allen's voice curled up at the end of the exclamation and her smile grew bigger.

"You don't know Rachel," Sam said. She ignored Mrs. Allen's smirk. If the two of them had been alone, she might have told Gabe's grandmother that she wasn't jealous of Rachel.

Sam was afraid that Linc Slocum's spoiled little princess of a daughter would do something to hurt Gabe's feelings.

Sam peeked at Gabe from the corner of her eye. She got the feeling he understood her fears even without meeting Rachel.

"At any rate," Mrs. Allen continued, "I hardly think Linc knew that I was asking him to hold off on burning the stubble on his fields for just a week until the colt's been adopted and moved from the area." Mrs. Allen stared at Sam again. "Samantha, what have I said that has you so absolutely slack-jawed?"

"The smell of the fields burning," Sam said. "That's what's bringing back the memory of the fire and making the colt panic."

"Isn't that what I just said?" Mrs. Allen asked.

"You figured it out," Sam told her.

"Figured it out?" Mrs. Allen tilted her head to one side. "Samantha, it seems fairly obvious."

"It does now," Sam said, laughing. "Can I go call Brynna? And Dr. Scott?"

"Help yourself," Mrs. Allen said, waving Sam toward the house. "I'll stay here and see what Gabe and the horse have got up to."

The sky was black velvet, sprinkled with stars. Gabe and Mrs. Allen had spread a blanket beside the colt's corral and Sam sat between them as they watched the late August meteor showers.

"There goes another one," Sam said. As the meteor's silver trail left a glowing streak across the darkness, Sam couldn't help thinking of the Phantom.

"Doesn't all that vastness make you feel small?" Mrs. Allen asked them both.

Crickets chirped in the moment of silence, before Gabe shifted on the blanket and grumbled, "It makes me feel itchy."

"Itchy?" his grandmother asked.

"Yeah, and this other one's no better." Gabe jerked in annoyance and rubbed at his bare, bruised leg. "I don't know, it's like muscle spasms. Man! It's like I stuck my toe in a light socket."

In the darkness Mrs. Allen turned to Sam. She couldn't see Mrs. Allen's face well, but the set of her shoulders was tense and expectant.

It took Sam a second to realize Mrs. Allen hoped it was a good sign that Gabe was feeling anything in his legs. Did it mean the swelling around his spine was going down? That he might be getting better?

"I'm sorry it's so uncomfortable. These days, they discourage using knitting needles or coat hangers to scratch inside it, don't they?" Mrs. Allen sounded merely sympathetic.

She doesn't want to get his hopes up, Sam thought.

"No scratching with *objects*. They say if you scratch the skin and it gets infected, you'll delay recovery." Gabe seemed to be parroting something he'd heard in the hospital. "But they also say the cure is to elevate it over your head."

"Mmm, that would be awkward," his grand-mother put in.

"Listen, hear that?" Gabe asked.

A scraping sound came from the corral. Sam saw the colt's outline on the far side of his enclosure, but she couldn't tell what he was doing.

"I bet his burns are itchy," Gabe said.

"Poor baby," Sam said.

"He's not a poor baby," Gabe yelped. "He gets to scratch."

"Gabriel, quit squirming or go back to the house," Mrs. Allen said. "For heaven's sake, you're acting six instead of sixteen."

Sam refereed before grandmother and grandson began another squabble.

"But he is good at thinking like a horse," Sam defended Gabe. "He's got the colt leading pretty well, too."

Dr. Scott had started the colt, but when Gabe walked around the outside of the corral, Pirate fol-lowed, hardly noticing that Sam held the end of the lead rope attached to his halter.

Just the same, she and Gabe had been vigilant for smoke. Their senses couldn't match the colt's, but she hoped, if it wafted this way, she'd have enough warn-ing to get out of the corral. Pirate's frantic memories would crowd out any consideration for humans.

"I might be a vet," Gabe said quietly, "you know,

if pro soccer doesn't work out."

"You could do that," his grandmother said, and Sam heard the pride in her voice.

"There's another one!" Sam and Gabe said in unison, and as she thought of the silver stallion again, Sam began wondering about the hot springs and Pirate.

And then, amazingly, Gabe said, "Have you ever heard of hydrotherapy for horses?"

"Oh my gosh, I was just wondering about that!" Sam said.

"I'm just thinking, the smoke craziness is something he needs to get over. He'd relax in warm water and maybe, if he smelled the smoke while he was there, and nothing bad happened—"

"That's perfect. All their movements are slower in water. He can't run and fall and hurt himself." Sam realized Gabe was talking over her.

"—if we take the colt to those hot springs you—"

Sam wanted to clap her hand over Gabe's mouth so he couldn't say anything about her and the Phantom. She settled for shooting her elbow against his ribs and hoped Mrs. Allen wouldn't notice.

Gabe caught his breath in surprise, but got her message.

"The hot springs?" Mrs. Allen asked dubiously.

"They use whirlpools and hot tubs and stuff like that for athletes, and I was just thinking it might kind of soothe him," Gabe said.

Mrs. Allen chuckled. "He's a wild horse, children. He's not going to lean back and be calm in those hot springs."

"He might," Sam said. She didn't openly contra-dict the older lady, but reminded her, "That *is* where we found Faith with the Phantom."

"That's true," Mrs. Allen said, and despite the faint light, Sam saw her smile.

"Besides, it's a medieval cure for madness," Gabe said.

"Is it?" Mrs. Allen gasped.

"That's what I read."

"For a boy who claims not to be a good student, you do read a lot," Mrs. Allen teased him.

Maybe because she was glad Gabe read and remembered, Mrs. Allen agreed they could try taking the colt to the hot springs. Gabe and Sam would walk, but she would arrive early in the truck and park nearby.

"I'll stay in the truck and leave you three to your-selves," Mrs. Allen said, "but only if you do this my way."

"What's your way?" Gabe sounded suspicious.

"We can't go at sunrise or sunset. That's when other wildlife is likely to be there and I want to cut our odds of having that colt act up."

"That's a good idea," Sam said. She shivered at what could happen if the Phantom's herd came to drink when the colt was there.

"Is that all?" Gabe asked, looking up at his grandmother as she stood.

"That's all I can think of right this minute," she said. "But I reserve the right to add more rules later on." She gave a strong-minded nod. "Now I'm going back up to the house. Sam, do you need anything?"

"Mosquito repellent, or a snake bite kit?" Gabe suggested, looking around the empty ranch yard.

"I'll be fine, Mrs. Allen," Sam said, ignoring him.

"Gabriel, are you coming?" his grandmother asked.

"I'll be right behind you," he said. "You can have a head start."

"Honey." Mrs. Allen's voice was a moan of regret as he reminded her of her mistake.

"I'm kidding, Grandma," Gabe told her, and his tone said he was telling the truth.

"Well all right, then," Mrs. Allen said with a sniff. "Don't take too long."

"I won't," he said, but he stalled until he heard the iron gate creak and Sam knew he was up to something.

He didn't make her wonder for long.

"In about a half hour," Gabe said, "she'll be asleep, and if she's not, you can pretend you're in the kitchen for a snack."

Sam crossed her arms. "And if I go along with whatever this is, why will I really be there?"

Gabe made a bouncing movement against his crutches.

Sam could see this idea had really him excited, though he clearly didn't think his grandmother would approve.

"You'll be getting one of those big plastic bags she keeps for gathering leaves and stuff. I saw them in the pantry. Then you'll be folding it up real small to bring with us tomorrow."

"Why will I be doing that?" Sam asked.

Gabe rapped his knuckles against his cast. His mischievous smile showed even in the dark. "I don't want this thing to melt."

So he wanted to get in the hot spring with Pirate.

"I'm not sure this is a very good idea," Sam said.

"Maybe not," Gabe agreed, shrugging, "but if you think I'd miss a chance to tell the guys that I soaked in a Wild West hot tub with a mustang, you're the one who's *loco*."

## Chapter Sixteen ⌾

$\mathcal{E}$verything was ready for Sam and Gabe to lead the colt to the hot springs.

Following Mrs. Allen's rule, they'd waited until mid-morning, long past the time the wild creatures would have come to the hot springs to drink and distract the colt.

The downside to Mrs. Allen's rule was the temperature. It had already soared to one hundred degrees.

*Sweaty for life*, Sam thought as she fanned the bottom of her red-and-white sleeveless jersey to make a breeze on her hot skin. The jersey was a relic from her middle school basketball uniform, but it was the coolest thing she'd brought, and it would dry quickly after their dip in the hot springs.

She'd already snapped the rope on the colt's halter and Gabe stood ready to open the gate when a blue Mercedes sedan came snarling down the dirt road toward the ranch.

*No, no, no!* Sam would have shouted the words if she hadn't been standing next to the colt.

The car belonged to Linc Slocum, and Sam would bet Rachel Slocum was driving.

It only made sense. Rachel had finished her summer trips to Europe, Bermuda, and Africa. Now she was home and bored.

She'd heard there was a teenage guy at Mrs. Allen's house—more importantly, a guy who hadn't yet fallen worshipping at her feet—and Princess Rachel had decided to remedy that situation.

Sensing Sam's agitation, the colt backed against the rope until he'd used up every inch of slack.

"It's okay, good boy," Sam whispered. "You're safe. After letting Tempest loose, she won't dare come near me or you. Not if she has any sense at all."

The mustang ducked his gleaming head and gave her a sidelong look from his white-patched eye.

"Yeah, I know," Sam whispered. "That part about her having good sense was a dumb thing to say, wasn't it?"

"When you two are done gossiping, maybe you can tell me who this is?" Gabe said, tugging at the collar of his faded blue T-shirt with the sleeves hacked off at the shoulders.

Sam guessed Gabe was wishing he'd worn something nicer for his trip to the hot springs. Not that it mattered. If Rachel flirted with him, she wouldn't care what he was wearing. He'd only be required to keel over at her beauty.

"Rachel Slocum," Sam muttered. "She's really rich and really pretty. She's never wanted anything her daddy didn't get for her but she—" Sam drew a deep breath. How could she explain? "In spite of her looks, Rachel Slocum is a witch."

Nervous as he was, Gabe laughed.

"I know the type," he said confidently, and for a few minutes, Sam thought he might be immune.

When Rachel steered the Mercedes off the driveway and through a neglected flowerbed, nearly ramming into Mrs. Allen's truck, Gabe laughed even harder. His chest shook so much, he had to regrip his crutches to keep from falling.

But when Rachel eased from the Mercedes, model-sleek in a bare-shouldered dress of floaty black and dusty orange tiers, Gabe's laughter stopped.

The dress would have looked like a Halloween costume on anyone less perfect, Sam thought, and wondered how this could possibly be fair.

"Sa-*man*-tha!" Rachel called, finger-combing a wave of mink-brown hair back from one eye.

*You've got a choice*, Sam told herself. She could release her fury in a scream at Rachel—which would be satisfying but would cost her every minute of progress she'd made with the colt — or she could pretend Rachel didn't exist.

"I don't hear a thing, sweet boy," she crooned to the horse.

"And you must be Gabriel." Rachel's voice was a purr. Even though she wore high-heeled sandals that wrapped her feet and ankles in complicated crisscrosses, she arrived at Gabe's side before he knew what was happening.

If she'd felt generous, Sam would have given Rachel credit for slinking so gracefully and quickly across the ranch yard, and for ignoring Gabe's crutches. But when Rachel tapped her little black envelope of a purse on Gabe's shoulder and he smiled a cocky grin that said he was totally taken in by her flirting, Sam felt a little sick.

"Hello, honey," Mrs. Allen said, approaching from the direction of her truck. Then, even though it was obvious, she asked, "What brings you all the way out here?"

Pirate's nostrils flared and his eyes widened. He could have scented Rachel's perfume, or maybe smoke from the Slocums' fields clung to Rachel's expensive clothes.

"Shhh," Sam told the colt. "She'll be gone soon."

"Actually, Mrs. Allen, I heard a snippet of gossip about your grandson," Rachel admitted with a giggle.

"Yeah?" Gabe said, encouraging her.

"I heard you looked like an angel, but you weren't. What about that?"

*Oh my gosh.* Sam wanted to demand Rachel's source, but this wasn't journalism class. Besides, Rachel had probably made up the comment because it was the sort of thing guys liked to hear about themselves.

Sam risked a quick glance at the two of them. Judging by the look on Gabe's face, Rachel was right.

"And the other reason, dear?" Mrs. Allen said.

It took Rachel a minute to answer and Sam was amazed to see a kind of dreamy look on the rich girl's face.

"Oh, yeah," Rachel said, shaking her head as if she'd shake off her softened mood. "I want to buy that horse my brother rode in that race."

"Roman?" Mrs. Allen asked, amazed.

"I guess," Rachel said.

*That horse. That race.* Rachel definitely wasn't focused on her errand.

Sensing no threat from the new human, Pirate stretched his muzzle out to nudge his bucket of Kool-Aid.

Sam knew she'd be overdoing it to call this love at first sight, but something was sizzling between Rachel and Gabe.

"This is a sports injury, I bet," Rachel said. She tucked her purse under one arm and flicked her manicured nails toward his legs. "Football?"

Gabe shook his head.

"Basketball?" she teased, and as she pretended to dribble a ball, her hand grazed his arm.

*Just go away,* Sam thought, but Rachel wasn't nearly as sensitive to telepathy as animals were.

Mrs. Allen stood frozen and Sam wondered if they were both thinking the same thing. If Gabe told the truth, Rachel would probably recoil. He'd only known her a couple minutes, so in one sense, it would-n't matter at all. In another way, it mattered a lot.

Suddenly the colt kicked at the soccer ball Gabe had left in his corral and Gabe looked up. He blinked. His cocky grin faded. Sam saw him decide to test Rachel and himself.

"Car accident," he said, and when Rachel licked her heavily glossed lips, he added, "I was in a coma for a while and they're not sure when I'll be able to walk, you know, in a regular way."

She snatched her hand back. The smile on her glossy lips was melting. The bright interest in her eyes grew faint.

"I'm sorry," Rachel said, and Sam was amazed to hear the sincerity in her voice.

"Yeah, me too," Gabe said, and his voice seemed to break the spell that, for a second, had made Rachel act like a genuine human being.

"I'd better be going," Rachel said and her eyes darted down to Gabe's legs, frankly staring this time. Gabe's jaw jutted forward and his eyes narrowed before he asked, "What about the horse for your brother?"

"Oh, I think that was a mistake," Rachel said. She sucked in a breath that seemed to shiver. "Sometimes I make the silliest mistakes."

She talked herself out of it, Sam thought as Rachel hurried back to the Mercedes. She liked him and he liked her, but he was less than perfect.

Sam glanced at Gabe. He must be fighting to keep his expression bored as Rachel backed the car and swung it the way she'd come.

Sam wished there was a way to tell Gabe how gutsy she thought he was for being honest, but how could she say it?

*Good thing you found out in the first ten minutes that Rachel Slocum doesn't follow her heart?*

What *did* Rachel follow? Sam couldn't even guess.

Gabe cleared his throat loudly, then blurted, "Too high-maintenance for me."

"Whatever do you mean?" Mrs. Allen asked her grandson.

"My school in Denver has a few millionaires' daughters, too," he said. "Girls like that never get tired of having you spend money on them."

Mrs. Allen looked confused, then her expression turned to one of understanding. It was less painful for Gabe to mention how materialistic Rachel was than to comment on Rachel's inability to like a guy on crutches.

"Can we go now?" Gabe asked.

"Certainly, but before we do, you two have to agree to one more rule," Mrs. Allen said.

"Okay," Sam said, and when her eyes met Gabe's she could see he was equally surprised that Mrs. Allen had been thinking about anything besides Rachel.

"If the colt should get loose, you're to let him go." Mrs. Allen shook an index finger in Sam's direction, but her glance swept over Gabe, too. "No heroic attempts to recapture him from either of you, is that understood?"

They both nodded, but as Mrs. Allen hurried toward her car, Gabe muttered, "If he tried to run, could you hold him?"

A far-off cicada whirred as Sam stared at him in disbelief.

"You know that expression, 'Wild horses couldn't drag me away'? Well, let me tell you, that was obviously made up by someone who's never been on the other end of the lead rope when a wild horse starts running."

## *Chapter Seventeen* ☙

*Carried away*, Sam thought as she and Gabe sandwiched the colt between them and set off.

She'd been carried away by the idea of taking the colt to the hot springs and she hadn't thought enough about the "what ifs."

Everything was fine now, as they crossed the bare ground around Deerpath Ranch, headed toward the sagebrush and sticker bush–studded fields of the shortcut to the hot springs. The colt stepped carefully and slowly through the vegetation. Every few steps, he turned his head away from her to nudge Gabe's shoulder.

But what if he caught the scent of smoke and went *loco*? What if he saw wild horses running and dragged her across the desert at the end of this lead rope? What if a sage hen burst from cover in front of him and he spooked, injuring Gabe?

"There are lots of sounds out here once you listen, huh?" Gabe said.

Sam listened. Ahead of them, Mrs. Allen's truck rolled slowly over the dirt road that ended about a quarter mile from the hot springs. Its tires spun monotonously, but crows cawed, too, and insects buzzed.

"Yeah, you're right," Sam said. There was no sense dumping all her misgivings on him. He had enough to worry about.

The colt stopped, raised his head, and snorted. Nostrils trembling, he tested the air.

"What do you think he smells?" Gabe asked.

"I think he's just recognizing this area," Sam said. "It's part of the Phantom's territory."

Sam couldn't believe Mrs. Allen had given permission to walk into this kind of danger. The colt had already proven he had memories. Who could blame him for wanting to return to freedom?

But maybe she was wrong. Maybe he wasn't searching for the scent of his wild herd, or recalling the nights he'd galloped in the dark of the moon with his family, pressed shoulder to warm shoulder, sleek side to side, to the river. He would have been a long-legged foal in the days that Mrs. Allen's fences were down and mustangs had grazed in her abandoned hay fields.

"Hey, buddy, you're okay," Gabe said, balancing to reach up and touch the colt's neck.

The colt trembled. He jerked his head up but didn't move away from Gabe.

*This rope won't hold him if he wants to go,* Sam thought again. She gave it another wrap around her hand, glad the colt's halter was soft cotton, and snug, so it wouldn't rub his healing burns.

From the tips of his ears, down his neck to the sweat-damp hair on his chest, the colt shook as if he were cold. His front hooves tapped in—what? Impatience? Confusion? Or maybe anticipation. Sam couldn't tell, but she knew some horses found water irresistible. Remembering this colt in the lake at War Drum Flats, she hoped that was what he was feeling.

"What do you think's got him so excited?" Gabe asked.

"He likes water," she said. "I think that's it."

"You don't think he wants to return to his herd?" Gabe asked as Pirate resumed walking.

Sam sighed, waited until a crow quit cawing nearby, then said, "That could be it, but you know, even if this hadn't happened to him, he would've been out on his own pretty soon, anyway."

"Why? All this stuff you've been telling me about herd animals—"

"Is true, but the lead stallion kicks out the young

males when they get to an age that . . ."

"They're too rowdy?" Gabe suggested.

"Well, sort of," Sam laughed. "But once they're on their own, they usually hang around in bachelor bands."

"That doesn't sound all bad," Gabe said, and Sam wondered if he was thinking of his own friends.

The colt bolted forward a few steps and the lead rope jerked painfully tight around Sam's hand.

"Shoot, five years of weight lifting and what good is it?" Gabe snapped. He gripped his crutches harder and rolled the muscles in his shoulders. "If I could just get rid of these crutches, I could hold him better than you can."

The colt's hooves stuttered to a stop. Wide-eyed, he scanned the desert.

"No offense," Gabe added as if he'd just heard what he'd said.

Sam brushed the apology aside.

"If he tries to go, don't even think about trying to stop him. He could drag either one of us to death."

"That's kinda harsh," Gabe said.

"That's the truth," Sam said, but suddenly her hands were shaking. She couldn't tell Gabe the nightmarish choice that had just occurred to her, so she kept talking. "If you tried to stop him, it wouldn't change anything—except you might get hurt and it might take you longer to get well. He'd still have to be recaptured by BLM."

And if BLM couldn't find him, Sam thought, would she help?

"It's kinda sad," Gabe said.

Sam stepped out to the end of the lead rope, then looked back at Gabe.

"Keep walking," she told him. "And we'll follow you. It's not nearly as sad as him suffering through a muddy autumn and snowy winter only to die when it gets too cold for his lungs."

"Wow," Gabe said. "Now I smell it, too. Smoke."

Gabe didn't stop. Now that he'd adapted his gait to the colt's, he swung along without pause.

Though she admired his determination, Sam couldn't help but wonder if the soft flesh under his arms wasn't rubbed raw with all the activity of the last few days. And when the colt swung his head to the side, giving Gabe a companionable nudge, Sam saw Gabe put his right leg down for balance.

It was getting better, she thought, but then Gabe noticed the direction her eyes had darted.

"Don't say anything," he ordered her. "Or you'll jinx me."

"Okay," she said.

"Pretend nothing's changed. It's up to the doctor to tell me if it's really better."

"I don't know what you're talking about," Sam said, shrugging, but excitement spurted through her veins.

\* \* \*

With only a short distance left before they

reached the hot springs, Sam decided there were no wild horses around. She hadn't seen a puff of dust or heard a clack of hooves on rock to support last night's fears.

In the darkness, she'd thought of riding while she led Pirate. Even though he wasn't used to it, she'd thought it might give her greater control. But then, it had occurred to her that even though summer was ending and mustang stallions had assembled their herds months ago, the Phantom might be lured to investigate a mare.

And once he'd come sniffing around Calico or Ginger, he might have recognized Pirate and taken him back to his secret valley.

Sam bit the inside of her cheek. Hard. She had to quit this. She wasn't being cautious. She was depressing herself to the point where she felt like she stood at the bottom of a cold, dank well.

"Hey, are you shivering, too?" Gabe asked. "It's about two hundred degrees out here!"

"I'm fine." Sam tried to keep her tone light. "You know that expression—like when you get chills for no reason, you say a goose walked over your grave?"

"Never heard that one, cowgirl," he joked. But Sam barely managed a smile. If the Phantom took the colt to his secret valley, BLM wouldn't find him. If she had to choose between revealing the Phantom's hiding place and letting this colt brave winter in the mountains and die, what would she do?

Tires skidded on dirt. They all looked ahead to see Mrs. Allen parking the truck.

They'd walk down to the hot springs, where the tumble of rocks would block them from her sight.

Sam looked back over her shoulder to see Mrs. Allen give a stiff wave.

*She's trusting me,* Sam thought.

"Wow! This is so outstanding!" Gabe said suddenly. "How could I have missed this?"

The hot springs sat like a vivid jewel amid the buff-colored dirt, weeds, and rocks. Pale aqua in the shallows darkened to turquoise, then dark jade green in the center.

"How deep is it?" Gabe asked.

"I don't know for sure, but not that deep, I don't think." Sam knew she sounded vague and distracted, but she couldn't quit scanning the area around them for anything that might frighten the colt.

"I've got to sit down," Gabe said.

"What's wrong?" Sam asked. The colt had quit trembling and Sam turned her worried gaze on Gabe.

"No big deal," he said, lowering himself to sit on a flat-topped boulder. "I just want to take a look at the path." He nodded toward the water. "Kind of strategize my way down there so the tips of the crutches don't slip or something."

If Gabe did fall, if he slammed face first into the rocks . . .

"Will you quit freaking out?" Gabe asked. His voice was low and almost kind.

"I'm not—"

"Sam, I can see you obsessing over what's going to happen. Shake it off."

Silence surrounded them.

Finally, Gabe shrugged. "Face it, if anything goes wrong, I did it to myself."

"That helps a lot," Sam snapped.

"Just figure out how you're going to get that plastic bag out of your pocket without him getting scared."

Sam drew a deep breath, and suddenly the moment came. A black bird with a flash of yellow on its wing sat wobbling on a reed. The colt snorted and took a step forward.

While he was distracted by the flutter of the bird's sudden flight, Sam dug her fingers into her back pocket and dropped the folded black plastic near Gabe.

As he pulled it up over his cast, it rustled, but the colt watched without shying.

"I don't think you have any idea how incredible this horse is," Sam told Gabe. "He's bonding to you. He's going to turn to you if something goes wrong."

"No he won't," Gabe said. He knotted the yellow

plastic drawstring with an adamant jerk. "He's more wild than he is mine."

The words hung between them for a minute before Sam smelled the smoke.

The hot air was clear, with no sign of drifting smoke, but the smell of it filled the air as strongly as if she'd been sitting in front of a fireplace.

The colt wasn't afraid. He straightened, ears pricked. His lips moved as if he were talking to himself. Then he licked his lips.

"What's he doing?" Gabe asked.

"I have no idea. That licking is supposed to be submissive, but—" Sam broke off, shaking her head.

All at once, the horse shook like a dog and the lead rope swung crazily, hitting Gabe and Sam before the colt surged forward toward the water.

"We're going in!"

Sam splashed along in the colt's wake as he pawed at the warm water, splashing his chest and his legs. She stayed steady on her feet as he lowered his face and, mouth open, splashed himself some more.

"He loves it!" Gabe shouted.

"You don't have to tell—" Sam began, but then the colt lowered himself into the hot springs.

*Warm as a hot tub*, she thought, but then the colt rolled onto his side and a wave of desert water hit her face, her jersey, and her shorts, drenching her completely.

Through wet eyelashes, Sam saw a blurry vision of Pirate tucking his legs in like a dozing colt.

*Horse island,* she thought, when only part of him showed above the blue water. Could he be floating? Or was his side resting on the bottom?

Blinking and wiping her eyes with the back of her free arm, she held tighter to the lead rope and didn't venture closer. If the colt decided to get his legs back under him, he'd thrash and cause such a commotion, he could hurt her without meaning to.

Then, he *was* thrashing, heaving himself over to wet his other side.

"Wait for me," Gabe said.

From the corner of her eye, Sam saw him sitting, easing one leg into the hot springs.

Coughing against a mouthful of warm water, Sam tried to be mad at Gabe for not understanding this was really a dangerous situation. But she couldn't be angry because she was delighted, too.

The gleaming colt groaned with pleasure, rolling his eyes and baring his teeth in contentment. He stayed on his side long enough that the water around him calmed to small ripples.

Gabe dangled his bruised leg within inches of the colt and Sam felt her heart tighten. The expression of bliss on the colt's face and Gabe's were identical. What could she do to convince him they were good for each other? No, it was more than that. They were *made for each other.*

But she didn't have to say a thing.

Eyes wide open, the colt lifted his scarred head and opened his mouth.

He wasn't going to bite Gabe. Sam knew that from his gentle expression, but Gabe didn't. His eyes widened in fear, but still he didn't move, so he was perfectly in position when the colt gave him a pink-tongued lick.

## *Chapter Eighteen*

"Did he just lick me?"

"Yeah," Sam said past her smile. "Some horses do that."

A sigh rolled through the colt and Sam's cheeks ached from the width of her grin. It didn't stop there, either. It spread, warming her in a way that had nothing to do with the hot springs or the hundred-degree day.

These two were healing each other. They had to stay together.

"He's your horse, you know," Sam said.

This time, Gabe didn't protest.

"I know. I guess I could keep him at Grandma's."

"Forget it," Sam said, surprised her whisper could sound so sharp. "You'd break his heart all over again."

Adopt him and leave? Think about that, Gabe."

"I don't know."

"Don't tell me there aren't stables in Denver," Sam said.

This time the big sigh came from Gabe. "Actually, there's a field right down the street. The guy who owns it lives next door, and he doesn't do anything with it. He keeps saying he's going to put in a swimming pool or something."

Gabe leaned over to rub the colt behind one ear. "Would you like that, Firefly? Huh, boy? Your very own swimming pool?"

Sam sat very still. Her hand tightened on the lead rope as it floated.

"Yeah, well," Gabe said. "I guess my secret's out. I've been calling him that in my head for a couple days."

"Firefly?" Sam said carefully.

"Okay, you might think this is totally sappy, but if you laugh, I don't care. And neither does he."

She didn't tell him she wouldn't laugh. He could have called this horse anything and she wouldn't have laughed. Naming the colt meant Gabe really had claimed him for his own.

"It has nothing to do with the bug," Gabe said. "It's more what a firefly looks like. Like a spark floating away from the fire. Escaping." Gabe's voice turned husky and even more quiet. "It's like the fire came after him, but it didn't get him. He made it. And he's going to be okay."

A sigh rocked the horse and a sense of peace fell over the hot springs.

Then Sam realized the birds were no longer squabbling. She didn't hear the buzzing of insects, either.

Her shoulders tightened. Why were all the desert creatures quiet?

All she heard was a faint wisp of country music from Mrs. Allen's truck radio and the crunch of dry weeds.

The colt jerked Sam farther into the hot springs as he rolled into a resting position, but he wasn't resting.

He struck out with a foreleg, trying to stand.

"Gabe, watch out!"

The colt lurched with a grunting effort. Then all four hooves were planted on the sandy bottom of the spring.

His ears twitched forward, then sideways. His eyes widened and his mouth gaped as he used every sense to interpret what had disturbed him.

Backing onto the shore, Sam stayed low, wrapping the rope around her hand. She planted her shoes on the driest rock she could see, and was looking around for another when Gabe spotted the Phantom.

"It's that stallion. He came for Firefly."

Peering through the reeds, Sam saw him, too.

"Maybe he just came to drink," she said, but none of them believed that.

The stallion pawed, creating a dust cloud that

made him ghostly, even in the heat of the day.

He tossed his head and the colt answered the summons with all his power.

"Chase him away!" Gabe pleaded.

But the colt slammed to the end of the rope. He bucked and his mane shone like a sheet of black satin.

The small bones in Sam's hand grated and she cried out as the rope tightened.

She couldn't hold him. She wanted to unsnap the lead rope, but she couldn't reach him. Sam opened her fingers at the same time that the colt flung himself sideways. With a mighty jerk, he ripped the rope from her hand.

Sam fell to her knees, holding the hand up to her mouth, gasping but still watching the colt.

The Phantom flattened his ears and swung his head at the colt.

He stopped. Though he was used to the stallion's superiority, the colt had clearly expected to be welcomed. He hesitated until the stallion's mouth opened and his teeth flashed.

It was a serious warning. Sam knew it even before the stallion reared and the sun made a silver corona of his flying mane.

The colt lowered his head. His lips moved in a silent plea to rejoin the band. Sam felt her throat close in sympathy.

But the Phantom would have none of it. When the colt jostled forward, trying to look past the stallion for the herd, the Phantom squealed and lunged forward, striking the colt's shoulder.

Firefly shied, but not before the silver stallion dealt him a painful bite on the neck.

The colt began backing as the Phantom wheeled. Hind legs tense, tail flung high, one hind leg struck out with the kick, but the colt didn't see it.

He turned toward the hot springs, making his way back to Gabe.

Sam stared after the Phantom. He was leaving as quickly as he'd come.

Alabaster white in the searing sun, he galloped away. Sam swallowed hard. Brynna would proba- bly say the stallion had just been warning off an intruding male, but Sam didn't quite believe that. He'd given Firefly the push he needed to start a new life.

"Hey!"

The colt had returned to Gabe with such enthusi- asm, he'd knocked him down.

Gabe wasn't moving.

"Easy boy," Sam said. As she crept back toward the horse, she could hear Gabe talking to him.

"You don't need him, Firefly," he said. "You've got me."

Sam stood still, watching the colt lip Gabe's shirt. Finally Gabe rolled to one side. Even as he gathered his crutches and struggled to his feet, the colt stayed beside him.

\* \* \*

Sam, Gabe, and Firefly hiked to the spot where Mrs. Allen had parked. Her dark head nodded forward, then she jerked out of her doze.

Blinking, she watched them approach, but if Mrs. Allen wondered about Gabe's scuffed knee, she didn't have a chance to ask.

"Grandma, I need you to help me," Gabe said.

"Just ask, honey."

"Okay." Gabe's tone sounded as if he'd given her fair warning. "I want you to help me convince Mom and Dad to let me keep Firefly."

He squared his shoulders as if the name were magical.

Mrs. Allen accepted it without question. "I'll do what I can," she said. "But you know a wild horse, especially one traumatized like this, is going to take a lot of time and attention."

"I've thought about that," Gabe said. "And I've got the time. During soccer season, I usually run before school. Then, after school, I was at practice until it was too dark to see the ball. I think the coach will understand if I don't sit on the bench and watch practice. That doesn't mean I won't still go to the games."

Gabe stopped when he heard his grandmother sniff and dab at the corner of her eye.

"Of course I'll help you, Gabriel," she said.

As they followed Mrs. Allen's truck back to

Deerpath Ranch, Sam was grateful Gabe hadn't mentioned the Phantom to his grandmother, and she said so.

Gabe snorted. "He's vicious. I don't know why you like him so much."

"He wasn't trying to hurt Firefly."

"No, he was just setting up to kick out his brains!"

"He struck out with one leg," Sam explained. "I've seen him mad, and this wasn't it."

"Yeah," Gabe said, looking back over his shoulder. "Maybe."

Sam turned, too, but there was no sign of her horse.

"I think the Phantom did him a favor," Sam said, and she kept on, even when Gabe shook his head. "I think he was just telling Firefly to"—she searched for the right words—"get a life."

Gabe took a deep breath, then turned to face the colt.

Firefly lowered his head and stood quietly as Gabe skimmed his hands over the colt's healing burns.

"'Get a life,' huh?" Gabe whispered to the horse.

"Well, as long as I'm around, he's got one with me."

From
## *Phantom Stallion*
~ 19 ~
SECRET STAR

Tempest had discovered her own neigh, and she wasn't afraid to use it.

Sam tried to escape the blast of high-pitched sound by pressing her spine against the wooden boards of the box stall and her palms against her ears. It didn't help much, but finally, the black filly stopped to draw a breath.

"Enough, baby," Sam crooned. "All the other horses can hear you. They know you're the princess of River Bend Ranch."

Sam wished she could make Tempest understand, because any minute a movie star horse and his trainer would come driving over the bridge to River Bend. In a way, Tempest really was River Bend's princess, Sam thought. The filly's sire was the swift and powerful silver stallion known as the Phantom. No one could deny he was a king among wild horses.

Tempest's mother, Dark Sunshine, had roamed free as the Phantom's queen until she'd reluctantly chosen the ranch as the safest place for her filly.

Sassy and proud, Tempest seemed totally aware of her heritage, and with two celebrities on the ranch, the filly might not get all the attention she thought she deserved.

Now, even Dark Sunshine had had enough of Tempest's shrill neighs.

"Hey Sunny, you're not leaving me here alone with her, are you?" Sam called after the buckskin mare.

Dark Sunshine didn't glance back. Shaking her black mane so hard that half of it flipped from the right side of her neck to the left, the mustang mare slipped out of the box stall into the corral.

Sam told herself she only imagined Sunny's sigh at the peace and quiet of the grassy enclosure.

Hands on her hips, Sam surveyed her morning's work. She'd cleaned all the stalls in the barn, by raking out the soiled bedding and replacing it with sweet-smelling straw. She'd paid special attention to the big box stall where the star stallion would stay when he wasn't in the corral adjoining the one Tempest shared with her mother.

*Inez Garcia and Bayfire.* Excitement sprinkled

down on Sam like bright confetti. Having two Hollywood celebrities right here on the ranch was almost unreal. She could hardly believe Maxine Ely, her friend Jake's mom, actually knew Inez Garcia and had recommended she and her stunt stallion stay at River Bend Ranch for a couple days before shooting a scene in Lost Canyon.

Just two nights ago, Inez Garcia had called, after talking with Jake's mom. Sam wished she'd been the one to answer the phone, but Brynna had left the dinner table just as the phone rang, so she'd been the lucky one.

"The rest of the crew is staying in Alkali," Brynna had said, after she'd explained the other details. Then she'd looked at Sam and added, pointedly, "but Inez would like BayFire's time here to be private."

Sam knew she'd sucked in a loud, disappointed breath before she blurted, "Does that mean I can't tell anyone?"

"That's right," Brynna had said. "Not even Jen." And there hadn't been a minute for negotiation.

"Where on earth will we put a movie star?" Gram had said. She'd bolted to her feet and begun gathering dishes and clearing the table as if she needed to start preparing that instant.

"She'll stay in her camper," Brynna had said. "And she made it very clear, she's just a horse trainer. In fact, her concern is for her horse. She obviously loves him."

At that, Dad had laughed. "Who wouldn't? If I owned the highest paid stunt horse in America, I'd love him, too."

"Oh Wyatt," Brynna had said, making a gesture to brush aside Dad's cynicism.

Now, as fresh straw rustled under Tempest's hooves, Sam wondered if Dad was right.

"Well, I love you, whether you can do anything or not," Sam told Tempest.

She bent, grabbed a handful of straw and waved it to amuse the filly.

With a side swipe of her black muzzle, Tempest knocked the straw from Sam's hand. Then she stamped a front hoof, lifted her chin and tried to stare over Sam's head.

"Don't talk back to me, young lady," Sam said, trying not to laugh at the filly's pose.

Maybe Tempest was bored with Sam's lecturing. Maybe she'd snuffled up dust that hadn't settled from Sam's raking. Whatever the reason, the filly began snorting and rolling her eyes.

As if he thought the foal's shrill neighs were about to start up again, Blaze, the ranch Border collie, gave a quick yap and bounded out of the barn.

In response, the filly gave a teeter-totter kick toward the barn's rafters. When Sam didn't scurry away, too, Tempest's ears pricked forward and her brown eyes turned studious.

Sam tightened her stubby ponytail. Then, arms

hanging loose from the short sleeves of her faded pink tee-shirt, legs relaxed in her jeans and boots, she tilted her head to one side.

*Loosen up and settle down*, her body language told the filly, and as she watched Tempest watch her, Sam fought back a yawn.

Tempest wasn't the only noisy one today.

The morning sky had been more black than blue when Sam had first looked out her bedroom window to see why a blue jay wouldn't stop squawking.

Finally she'd spotted a winged shadow dive-bombing Cougar, her tiger-striped cat, as he tried to slink across the ranch yard.

Cougar must have slipped outside at Dad's heels, without him noticing, because the cat wasn't allowed outside the house during the hours coyotes might be around. But the ranch was a compact little world of its own, and nothing stayed secret for long.

"You're caught," Sam had said through the window pane, though there was no way the cat could hear her.

As the cat and bird had moved farther from the two story white ranch house, Sam had climbed back into bed, hoping for a few more minutes of sleep.

It hadn't worked. Just seconds later Brynna's hairdryer began howling from the bathroom down the hall.

Even though it was Saturday, her stepmother and Gram had risen early, rushing to do some errands in

Darton before Inez Garcia and Bayfire arrived.

Sam had pulled the pillow over her head, trying to drown out the sound, but then the vacuum cleaner had started droning downstairs.

Though Inez Garcia had insisted she didn't want any special treatment, Sam wasn't surprised by Gram's last minute housekeeping.

Gram had probably baked something delicious, too, but if so, she'd hidden it. When Sam made her way down into the kitchen for breakfast, Gram and Brynna were gone and she'd been left with nothing but cold cereal and toast.

Tired of Sam's daydreaming, Tempest gave a low nicker.

"Save your voice." Sam coaxed the filly. "I've had enough noise this morning."

As if Sam had thrown down a dare, Tempest extended her tiny muzzle upward and released another ear-splitting whinny.

Over the foal's noise, Sam heard hammering and a rumble outside the barn. Dad was starting up his new tractor.

Sam sighed. She guessed she should go out and admire the machine, even though she didn't under-stand Dad's decision to buy it.

By entering a drawing at the rodeo, she'd won Dad a brand new truck equipped with every luxury imaginable. Besides its off-road ability, the truck had a windshield tinted to cut the glare of the desert sun, heated seats to warm predawn trips out to break the ice off the cattle's water, and a sound system that surrounded you with music real enough that you might have been onstage with the band.

But Sam only knew this from the brochure that had come with the winner's certificate. Dad had turned down the truck.

Instead of starting it up shouting "yippee" all the way home, he'd made an agreement with the truck dealer. Dad had traded in his old tractor and truck. Their value, added to the price of the prize truck, had equaled the cost of a six-year-old steel gray truck, which was nice enough, and a state-of-the-art tractor that did everything, he said, except plant the hay and sell it to the highest bidder.

"I'm out of here," Sam told the filly.

Tempest stopped neighing and followed so close that Sam felt the warmth of the filly's body. Then, Tempest wiggled her head between Sam's side and arm, forcing a hug.

Smiling, Sam turned to face her.

Looking up from under long eyelashes, the filly gazed into Sam's face.

"Could you be any cuter?" Sam asked.

The tension in Sam's shoulders and the ringing in her ears vanished.

She'd never believed she could love another horse as much as she did Ace and the Phantom, but her heart had room for one more.

Sam hugged Tempest's neck, then lowered her lips to the filly's cupped black ear and whispered, "Xanadu."

The name was their secret. Sam never stopped imagining where the mythical place called Xanadu might be. Was it the secret valley where the Phantom kept his herd, an invisible place that hovered here between them, or someplace she and the filly had yet to discover together?

"That's what I hope," Sam said.

# Read all the Phantom Stallion Books!

www.phantomstallion.com

**#6: The Challenger**
Pb 0-06-441090-0

**#7: Desert Dancer**
Pb 0-06-053725-6

**#8: Golden Ghost**
Pb 0-06-053726-4

**#4: The Renegade**
Pb 0-06-441088-9

**#5: Free Again**
Pb 0-06-441089-7

**#1: The Wild One**
Pb 0-06-441085-4

**#2: Mustang Moon**
Pb 0-06-441086-2

**#3: Dark Sunshine**
Pb 0-06-441087-0

**#9: Gift Horse**
Pb 0-06-056157-2

**#10: Red Feather Filly**
Pb 0-06-056158-0

**#11: Untamed**
Pb 0-06-056159-9

**#12: Rain Dance**
Pb 0-06-058313-4

**#13: Heartbreak Bronco**
Pb 0-06-058314-2

**#14: Moonrise**
Pb 0-06-058315-0

**#15: Kidnapped Colt**
Pb 0-06-058316-9

**#16: The Wildest Heart**
Pb 0-06-058317-7

**#17: Mountain Mare**
Pb 0-06-075845-7

**AVON BOOKS**

*An Imprint of HarperCollinsPublishers*